The Fiends of
NIGHTMARIA

The Fiends of NIGHTMARIA

STEVEN ERIKSON

TOR

A TOM DOHERTY ASSOCIATES BOOK
NEW YORK

THE FIENDS OF NIGHTMARIA

Copyright © 2016 by Steven Erikson

A Tor Book
Published by Tom Doherty Associates
120 Broadway
New York, NY 10271

www.tor-forge.com

Tor® is a registered trademark of Macmillan Publishing Group, LLC.

The Library of Congress Cataloging-in-Publication Data is available upon request.

ISBN 978-1-250-76814-8 (trade paperback)
ISBN 978-0-7653-2427-6 (hardcover)
ISBN 978-1-250-76815-5 (ebook)

Our books may be purchased in bulk for promotional, educational, or business use. Please contact your local bookseller or the Macmillan Corporate and Premium Sales Department at 1-800-221-7945, extension 5442, or by email at MacmillanSpecialMarkets@macmillan.com.

Originally published in the United Kingdom by PS Publishing

First U.S. Edition: March 2021

The Fiends of
NIGHTMARIA

Part One

ONE NIGHT IN FARROG

Beetle Praata's horse collapsed under him just outside the embassy's stables, making it easier to dismount. He stepped to one side to regard the fallen beast, and then gave one tentative kick to its lathered haunch, eliciting no response.

Puny Sploor, the groundskeeper and stabler, edged into view from the sentry cubicle, holding one flickering candle, his rheumy eyes blinking.

Beetle Praata gestured at the horse. 'Brush this down and drag it close to some hay.'

Puny rubbed at one skinny arm, as if the effort of holding up the candle had exhausted it. 'It's dead,' he observed.

Beetle frowned and then shrugged. 'You never know.'

Leaving the stabler and the horse in the small yard, the Imperial Courier of Nightmaria made his way into the embassy. Just outside the heavy bronze door he paused and squinted up into the night sky. The stars seemed to swim in a vast pool of black water, as if he had sunk to unimaginable depths, swallowed by a diluvean dream from which no awakening was possible. He drew a deep, cleansing breath, and then lifted the heavy iron ring, turned it until it clicked, pulled open the massive door, and strode inside.

The air within was redolent, thick with the pungent reek of decay. Offering bowls of green, slimy copper occupied flanking niches at eye-level to either side of the formal entranceway, filled with moss from which parasitic flowers spilled down to snake across the narrow ledges. A thick, loose rug underfoot made wet sounds beneath his boots, and from it arose the cloying smell of rot.

He unclipped his scaled leather highway cloak, shaking the dust from it before setting it on a hook. He plucked from his belt a pair of kid-skin gloves and methodically pulled them on, ensuring that each finger was snug. Satisfied, he continued on, exiting the entranceway to find himself in the vast audience chamber that had never known a foreign guest. The lush padding of the settees to either side of the Ambassador's Chair were now lumpy, the filling spilled out from rotted holes here and there, and in places where small creatures nested the humps in the fabric moved up and down every now and then. Overhead, a chandelier of roseate crystal was mostly obscured beneath frayed braids of moss and lichens, its hundred candles long since eaten by mice and whatnot. From somewhere nearby, water trickled.

Beetle Praata strode to one side and tugged on a ratty cord, somewhat gingerly lest it part, and upon hearing a distant chime, he nodded to himself and settled in to wait.

Motion from beneath one of the settees drew his eye and he observed as a slow-worm, with a blunt maw big enough to swallow the head of a small dog, slithered into view. Lifting its sightless muzzle, it quested from one side to the next, and then set out sliding directly towards Beetle.

From somewhere nearby, deeper into the sanctum, came a

muted dragging sound, along with faint, meaty flops, and the hint of something scaly sliding across the damp tiles.

Beetle crouched when the slow-worm finally reached him. He patted its blunt head, lightly enough to keep the stains to his gloves to a minimum. The slow-worm circled him, its knobby tail twitching. As the other sounds drew closer, he straightened and turned in time to see a hunched, un-even form creep into view from a narrow passageway hidden behind a mouldy curtain.

Clad in green silks, Ambassador Ophal D'Neeth Flatroq seemed to hover a moment, and then began a rhythmic sway-ing, similar to a cobra with hood unfurled. The robe Ophal wore was high-cowled, framing a bald pate of glistening scales, strangely curled ears that ended at vague, possibly chewed points, eyes of murky green, pallid brows and cheeks the hue of a serpent's belly, and a toothless mouth of thick, flabby lips. One hand held up an open oil lamp, flames flicker-ing, revealing fingers without nails and heavy scales upon the back of the hand.

A thin tongue slipped out and darted for a moment before retreating again.

Beetle Praata bowed. 'Ambassador.'

'Hissip svlah, thlup?'

'Alas, yes. As expected, I'm afraid.' The Imperial Courier reached beneath his tunic and drew out a wooden tube, its ends sealed in wax, the seals bearing the stamp of the Royal Signet Ring.

'Prrlll obbel lell,' Ophal sighed, placing the oil lamp on a nearby ledge and then accepting the king's command. Twist-ing one end of the tube broke a seal and the ambassador probed with a greenish finger until he was able to pull out the vellum. Unfurling it, Ophal peered close, eyes tracking the script. His tongue slithered out again, this time from one corner of his mouth, then retreated once more. 'Ahh, prrlll. Flluth villl rrrh na.'

Beetle's brows lifted. 'This very night? Very well. Shall I await the reply?'

Ophal nodded, and then sighed again. 'Mah yull thelff hathome.'

The courier bowed a second time.

The ambassador gestured down at the slow-worm, 'Eemlee, prrlll come!'

Ophal retreated from whence he came, the slow-worm slithering after him.

Beetle walked over to one of the settees and carefully sat down, ensuring that he crushed nothing. It was going to be a long night. He watched a spider chase a mouse across the floor.

'We do it tonight,' said Plaintly Grasp, leaning over the ale-stained table, the one always reserved for her at the very back of Pink's Tavern. She ran a finger through a pool of ale, making a stream to the table's edge, and watched it drain.

'Hey,' growled Barunko, 'something's wet my crotch.' He straightened slightly, glaring about.

'You're always saying that,' observed Symondenalian Niksos—known to many as The Knife. He was playing with one of his daggers, the blade slipping back and forth and under and over his scarred, cut-up hand. The blade twisted and he winced, but continued his manipulations. 'Tonight, is it? I'm ready. I've been ready for a week.'

Scowling across at him, Plaintly said, 'She was arrested only two nights ago, you idiot. And stop that, you're dripping blood all over the table again.' She looked to the others. In addition to Barunko—their muscle—and Symondenalian Niksos, who couldn't recall seeing a back he didn't want to stab, there was Lurma Spilibus, who'd never met a lock she couldn't pick or a purse she couldn't snatch, her red tangle of curly hair piled high and wayward, her triangular face bulging at one cheek with a wad of pulped Prazzn, her eyes perpetually crossed as she squinted at the tankard cradled in her hands.

Beside Lurma and huddled together, Mortari and Le Groutt, master burglars who'd yet to meet a wall they couldn't scale. Mortari was the smaller of the two, with a pinched face and the manic eyes of a terrier needing to piss. He was panting slightly in the fug of the tavern. Leaning hard against his left shoulder was Le Groutt, swarthy and snaggle-toothed, showing his broad and possibly witless yellow grin, his head bobbing as he looked about, habitually assessing walls, railings, ledges and whatever else a man might climb.

She studied them all, gauging, and then nodded. 'So we're back together,' she said.

Le Groutt showed her his smile. 'The Famous Party of Five.'

'Infamous,' drawled Symon The Knife. He flinched and the knife clattered to the tabletop. Sucking at his thumb, he glowered at Plaintly but said nothing more.

'The Royal Palace,' mused Lurma. 'That won't be easy. Who knows what that insane necromancer's let loose in the crypts.' She snapped up her crazed squint, shifted the wad in her mouth until it bulged the other cheek, and then said, 'Barunko, you up to this? Could be demons. Revenants. Giant snakes.'

'Unsubstantiated,' cut in Plaintly. 'He's a usurper. That and nothing more. And the new Grand Bishop is a drooling simpleton. All this talk of sorcery and necromancy is just propaganda, to keep away people like us.'

'Did I pee on myself?' Barunko asked.

'He's arrested the Head of the Thieves' Guild,' Plaintly went on. 'Our Mistress. Now maybe it's been a few years since we all worked together, but we ain't lost a step, not one of us. There's nobody better in Farrog, and now the usurper's declared war on our guild. We're getting her out and we're doing it tonight. One more time, the finest adventuring band of thieves this world has ever seen. So,' she leaned back baring her teeth. 'Is everyone ready for this?'

'I've been ready for a week,' said Symon The Knife, collecting up his blade and twirling it one-handed, until it slipped from his grasp and embedded itself in Barunko's meaty thigh.

The huge man sat up straighter, looking around. 'We in a fight? Is this a fight? Let me at 'im!'

The broad, blustery face of Grand General Pin Dollop, Commander of the Royal Farrogal Army, beamed. 'Say what you like about this new king,' he said in a voice that should have been low and throaty, perhaps even a growl, but was instead thin and reedy, 'he understands the importance of protecting our borders.'

Seneschal Shartorial Infelance paced before the General in the cluttered Strategy Room, her silk robes swirling with restless motion. 'I think you need to explain this to me one more time, Dollop. How is it that raiding beyond those borders constitutes a defensive gesture? Think well on your answer. These are the Imperial caravans of Nightmaria your troops are savaging. Granted, we don't know much about the Fiends but all that we've heard bodes ill. Stirring up that nest seems precipitous.'

'Nonsense,' Pin Dollop replied. 'It's been too long we let those inhuman spawn squat nice and cozy in those mountain keeps, watching our every move from on high. The old king flinched at his own shadow. It was all appease this and placate that. Concessions on the tolls and tithes, all that merchant-ware skipping right past poor Farrog, making the Fiends filthy rich and us scraping the coffers year after year.' His small eyes tracked Shartorial Infelance. 'Now, this new king of ours, he's got spine. And the Grand Bishop's just this evening signed the Proclamation of Holy War against the Fiends of Nightmaria.' He made a fist and ground it into the cup of his other hand. 'Scour the scum from their caves! Roast their lizard hides on spits!'

Shartorial sighed. 'They've always respected the closed borders between us, General, and have made a point of hiding their hideousness through intermediaries—'

'Barring that slimy Ambassador of theirs!' Pin Dollop shivered. 'Makes my skin crawl and creep. Well, enough of that. We got us a real king now and I don't care how he got to the throne—tell me, are you mourning the old king? Honestly?'

Frowning, she shook her head. 'Not much, granted. But,' and she halted her pacing to face Pin Dollop, 'something about this new one . . .'

'Give him time. Besides,' the General rubbed at his jowls, 'the man sports a very fine beard. Very fine indeed.'

Shartorial's frown deepened as she studied the man. 'Well,' she allowed in a neutral tone, 'there is that.'

'Precisely. Anyway, the army's chewing at the bit. We'll field the whole complement. Five Legions, four thousand soldiers who've been training for this for months.' He made stepping motions with one hand. 'Up into the mountains, killing every damned Fiend we come across! Investing the keeps, burning them out and if that doesn't work, starving them out! I've waited my whole life for this! Conquest!'

She cleared her throat. 'Our defensive strategy.'

'In the name of security,' Pin Dollop said, wagging a finger, 'all measures are justified. Fiends skulking in shrubbery.

Unacceptable. You don't tolerate a viper's nest in your back-yard, do you? No, you burn it out, scour it clean, make the world a better place.'

'The citizens are certainly fired up,' Shartorial allowed.

'Exactly. Have we ever been so unified? No. Do recall, we came very near a civil war only three months ago! If not for the new king enforcing order, this city would be a shambles—and you can swear to the Indifferent God himself that the Fiends would have pounced!'

'General,' Shartorial Infelance said, 'I'd hardly call dissen-sion over this year's Artist of the Century a civil war.'

'Anarchy in the streets, Seneschal! The new king's first act was decisive.'

'He arrested all the artists.'

'A brilliant move! Enough of these stupid festivals and all those sniveling poets! They didn't have much to sing about writhing on spikes on the city walls, oh no, hah!'

Shartorial sighed again. 'It's late. When do you march?'

'Soon,' Pin Dollop promised. 'Let the Fiends quiver and shake in their slimy holes!'

'Indeed,' she replied. She left the General at his map-table, his fist grinding rhythmically in the cup of his other hand.

'The world is so unfair,' moaned Brash Phluster, trying to loosen his shoulders, but with the rack on the third notch there was little give. He whimpered. 'What time is it? Where's that Royal Torturer? He's late! Why's he always late? He's forgot-ten me! How could he do that? Whose turn is it? Who's next? Someone bribed the bastard, didn't they? Which one of you? You disgusting pieces of filth! Every one of you! Oh, it hurts!'

'You've been there for less than half a bell,' said Apto Can-avalian.

'It was you!' Brash accused, twisting about on the rack, turning his head in an effort to glare at the man chained to the wall to his right, but the angle was too sharp and spasms of agony lanced through his neck. 'Ow, you bastard!'

'I won't change my vote,' Apto taunted, rattling the chains. 'That's why I'm still alive. I'm too sane to kill, you see. For all the usurper's faults, he knows enough to admire a rational compatriot—'

'Shut your face,' growled Tiny Chanter. 'There ain't nothing rational about the Nehemoth. Tiny knows rational and this ain't it, they ain't it, you ain't it. Isn't that so, Midge?'

'It's so,' agreed Midge.

'Flea?'

'Yeah. So.'

'So shut your face, y'damned weasel. Besides, you know you're next on the rack, so it's not like you got no stake, is it? I know you're next cause I'm right after you—'

'No you're not,' said Midge. 'I am.'

'What? No, brother, I'm sure it's me. The fucking poet and then the fucking critic, and then Tiny Chanter.'

'I'm on the rack after Apto,' said Midge stubbornly. 'Then you, Tiny, and then Tulgord Vise—'

'What about me?' Flea demanded.

'You're after Steck Marynd, Flea, and he's not there long on account of his broke leg and all his screaming, and then it's back to the Century's Greatest Artist.'

'That title's a curse!' Brash Phluster hissed. 'Oh, this is what being an artist is all about, isn't it? You paying attention, critic? It's suffering, misery, torture! It's grief and pain and agony, all at the hands of people too dim-witted to appreciate talent, much less understand the sacrifices us poets make—'

'He hasn't killed you yet because he likes the joke,' cut in Apto Canavalian.

'*What joke?*' Brash screamed. 'Ow, it hurts to scream! Ow!'

'The joke,' the critic and short-lived guest judge in the Festival of Flowers and Sunny Days explained, 'that is you, of all people, winning the contest. Thief of talent, imposter and charlatan. This is the curse of awards. Their essential meaninglessness, their potential for absurdity and idiocy and crass nepotism—'

'Listen to you!' crowed Brash Phluster. 'Took so many bribes you bought a villa on the river-side!'

'That's right. I took them all, which in turn cancelled them all out, freeing me to judge on merit alone—'

'They arrested you before the vote! Before that necromancer murdered the king and took the throne!'

'And look at the hypocrisy of that fiasco!' Apto retorted. 'The same people calling for my head were the ones who bribed me in the first place!' He let out a long breath. 'Of course, it's my newfound wealth that permitted me to buy a day off from the rack. You've been doubled up, Poet. And why not? Like you said, artists suffer and so they should. Leeches on the ass of society, every one of you!'

'I knew it! Listen to him! Mister Bitter! Mister Envy!'

'Keep it up and I'll buy you another notch, Phluster.'

'You disgusting piece of filth! Death to the critic! Death to all the critics!'

'All of you,' grated Steck Marynd from across the chamber, 'be quiet. I'm trying to get some sleep here.'

Tulgord Vise cursed under his breath and then said, 'And so I am betrayed. By all of you! We should be planning our escape, not bickering about this and that. The Nehemoth now sits on the throne of this city, luxuriating in his evilness. We need to be devising our vengeance!'

'Tiny's got a plan,' said Tiny. 'Tiny goes on the rack all meek and nice. The Royal Torturer likes Tiny Chanter. It's all part of Tiny's plan.'

'Tiny's a nitwit,' said Apto Canavalian.

'When Tiny escapes,' growled Tiny, 'he leaves the critic behind.'

'Yes!' cried Brash Phluster.

'And the poet.'

'What? What have I ever done to you, Tiny? That's not fair!'

'We should've eaten you first on the trail,' said Tiny Chanter, shifting in his chains. 'Not those others. Instead, we'll just tighten things up another ten or so notches, ripping you apart. Pop! Pop, pop! Hah hah! Right, Midge?'

'Hah hah,' laughed Midge.

'Flea?'

'Why am I before the poet? I thought I was last!'

Emancipor Reese watched the headless corpse shuffle into the throne room bearing the gilded broken circle that symbolized the Holy Church of the Indifferent God, and a moment later the Grand Bishop strode in, dressed in heavy brocaded robes of vermillion and rose. He paused then, frowning as if ambushed by a sudden thought.

Clearing his throat, Bauchelain went on from his seat on the throne, 'Tyranny, as I was saying, Mister Reese, is a delicate balance between the surety of violence and the inculcation of passive apathy. The latter is presented as an invitation permitting a safe haven from the former. In short, keep your head down and your mouth shut, and you'll be safe. By this means one pacifies an entire population.'

Grunting, the Grand Bishop turned around and departed the chamber, the headless sigil-bearer turning and following.

Emancipor plucked a grape from the laden bowl beside his stool. He bit lightly and sucked out the juices before casting the wrinkled pulp into a spittoon at his feet. 'I get all that, Master. I was just saying how things have gotten kind of quiet, even boring, now that all the poets and singers and musicians and dancers are gone.'

'Art worthy of the name, Mister Reese, is the voice of subversion. Oh to be sure, there is a place for its lesser manifestations in the ideal civilization, as a source of mindless entertainment and, indeed, eager escapism. One can appreciate the insidious denial promulgated by such efforts. Dance and sing whilst everything falls to pieces and the like. Have you ever perused—carefully and with diligence—the face of an ecstatic dancer or reveler? In some, Mister Reese, you will find the bliss of a trance state, an elevation of sorts you might say. But in most, you can see the glimmer of fear. Revelry is a flight, a frenzied fleeing from the misery of daily existence. Hence the desperate plunge into alcohol and drugs, to aid that escape.'

Emancipor squinted up at Bauchelain, eyes narrow. 'Is that so?' he said, reaching quickly for his goblet of wine.

'Maintaining a state of pensive terror of course has its limits,' the new king of Farrog went on. 'Hence the identification and demonization of an external threat. At its core, Mister Reese, the notion of "us" and "them" is an essential component in social control.'

Draining the goblet dry, Emancipor reached for his pipe and began tamping it with rustleaf and d'bayang. 'The Fiends,' he said.

'Just so. Convenient, wouldn't you say, that our kingdom borders a xenophobic but wealthy mountain empire of unhuman lizard people? Such an enemy obviates the convoluted abuse of logic required to differentiate and demonize neighbors who are in fact little different from the rest of us. Hair color? Skin tone? Religious beliefs? Blue eyes? Yellow trousers? All patently absurd, of course. But unhuman lizard people? Why, could it be any easier?'

Emancipor lit his pipe and drew hard. 'No, Master, I suppose not.' He blew out a cloud of smoke. 'Mind you, sir, I've got some experience when it comes to peering at maps and whatnot.'

'Your point?'

'Well, Master, it's this, you see. Blank patches, on maps, make me nervous. The Unknown Territory and all that. I've sailed plenty of seas, come up on those patches, and well, usually they're blank for a reason, right? Not that they're unexplored—there ain't nothing in this world that ain't seen some adventurer creeping in to see what there is to see. So, blank patches, sir, are usually blank because whoever went in never came back out.'

'You certainly become voluble, Mister Reese, once the d'bayang floods your brain, diminishing, one presumes, its normal addled state. Very well, I do concede your point.'

Emancipor glanced again at Bauchelain. 'Aye? You do?'

'Let it not be said that I am unreasonable. We have traveled in step for some time now, haven't we? Clearly we have come to know one another very well indeed.'

'Aye, Master,' said Emancipor, quickly reaching for the carafe of wine and topping up his goblet again. He downed three quick mouthfuls and then resumed puffing the pipe. 'Very well, uh, indeed.'

'General Pin Dollop, however, being a native of Farrog, speaks with certain familiarity regarding the Fiends.'

'Aye, Master, he's a man full of opinions, all right.'

Bauchelain smiled from his throne. 'Ah, do I sense some resentment, Mister Reese? That he should have ventured so close in my confidence? Are you feeling somewhat crowded?'

'Well, Master, it's only that I share the Seneschal's caution.'

'Ah, the lovely Shartorial Infelance. Of course, caution is an essential virtue given her responsibilities.'

'Caution,' Emancipor said. 'Aye.'

'Mister Reese, the Royal Treasury is somewhat bare.'

'Well, sir, that's because we've looted it.'

'True. However, tax revenues are down.'

'Aye, we've squeezed them dry.'

'Just so. Hence the pressing need for an influx of wealth. Tyrannies are expensive, assuming the central motive of being a tyrant king is, of course, the rapid accumulation of vast wealth at the expense of the common folk, not to mention the beleaguered nobility, such as it is.'

'I thought it was all about power, Master. And control. And the freedom to frighten everyone into submission.'

'Well, those too,' Bauchelain conceded. 'But these are only means to an end, the end being personal wealth. Granted, there is a certain pleasure to be found in terrorizing lesser folk. In unleashing a torrent of fear, suffering and misery. And let it not be said that I have been remiss in addressing such pleasures.'

'No, Master, not at all. Who'd ever say something like that?'

'Precisely. In fact, I would proclaim such bloodlust a potent symbol of my essential humanity.'

'Well, Master, let's hope those lizards don't share that particular trait.'

The headless sigil-bearer returned, and behind it the Grand Bishop. 'Bauchelain,' said Korbal Broach in his high, thin voice, 'I just remembered what I was coming here to tell you.'

'Most excellent, Korbal. Out with it, then.'

'That ferryman, Bauchelain. The one we put in the deepest dungeon.'

'Our possessed prisoner, yes, what of him?'

'He's dead.'

Bauchelain frowned. 'Dead? How did that happen?'

'I think,' said Korbal Broach, 'death by masturbation.'

Emancipor rubbed at his face. 'Well, of all the ways to go . . .'

'Very well,' said Bauchelain. 'I see. Ah, of course.'

Korbal Broach nodded. 'Not possessed any more, Bauchelain.'

'In other words, old friend, the Indifferent God has escaped his mortal prison, and now runs free.'

Korbal Broach nodded a second time. 'That's bad.'

'Indeed, very bad. Hmm.' Abruptly Bauchelain rose to his feet. 'Mister Reese, attend me. We shall retire to my Conjuration Chamber. It seems that on this gentle night, we must summon and unleash a veritable host of demons. Korbal Broach, do you sense the god's presence in the crypts?'

'I think so. Wandering.'

'Then a most lively hunt awaits us, how delightful! Mister Reese, come along now.'

Trembling where he sat, Emancipor Reese tapped out his pipe. 'Master, you wish me to help you raise demons? You never asked that of me before, sir. I think—'

'Granted, Mister Reese, I may have been remiss in neglecting to mention the possibility in our employment contract. That said, however, these are most unusual circumstances, would you not agree? Fear not, if by some mischance you are rent limb from limb, be assured it will be a quick death.'

'Ah, thank you, Master. That is . . .'

'Of some comfort? Happy to set you at ease, as ever, Mister Reese.'

Korbal Broach said, 'I'll raise the rest of my undead, Bauchelain.'

Bauchelain paused and studied his old friend. 'Any risk that one might be suborned?'

'No, Bauchelain. None of them have any heads.'

'Very good then. Well, on a hunt such the one awaiting us, the more the merrier. Mister Reese? Time's wasting!'

Mortari crouched in the shadows of the alley mouth, Le Groutt crowding his side. He peered at the high wall of Royal Palace. 'I see handholds,' he whispered.

'I see footholds,' Le Groutt whispered back.

'So, we got handholds and footholds.'

'Handholds and footholds.'

'Can't be done.'

'Not a chance.'

Together, they turned about and crept back to where waited the others. Mortari edged up close to Plaintly Grasp. He rubbed at his terrier face, scratched behind an ear, licked his lips and then said, 'Not a chance.'

'Not a chance,' chimed in Le Groutt, his large teeth gleaming.

'Unless Barunko can throw us high, up near one of the spikes,' Mortari said.

'Grab hold of the corpse's leg and hope it don't tear off,' added Le Groutt.

'Up past that . . .'

'Handholds and footholds.'

Sighing, Plaintly Grasp turned to Barunko. 'Well?'

'Throwing? I can throw. Give me something to throw.'

'You'll be throwing Mortari,' explained Plaintly. 'Up to one of those spikes.'

'Spikes?'

'The ones on the wall.'

'Wall?'

'Over there.' She pointed.

Barunko looked about. 'Wall,' he said, grunting. 'Show me.'

Symon The Knife spat onto the greasy cobbles. 'This is a problem,' he said.

'What is, Symon?' Plaintly demanded in a hiss. 'He said he can do it, didn't he?'

Drawing out a dagger, Symon gestured with it towards Barunko. 'Back when the Party of Five was the terror of the city's wealthy,' he said, 'our muscle here could still see past his own nose. Now, well . . .'

'It don't matter,' insisted Plaintly. 'We just point him in the right direction. Like we did on the last job—'

'Oh,' piped in Lurma Spilibus, 'the *last* job.'

'We survived it!' Plaintly snapped. She grasped Barunko by an arm and started dragging him towards the alley mouth. 'This way,' she said. 'You just grab Mortari and throw him as high as you can, right?'

'Throw Mortari,' Barunko said, nodding. 'Where is he?'

'I'm right here—'

Barunko spun, grasped hold of Mortari, and threw him across the street. The 2nd story man struck the palace wall with a meaty thud and then crumpled to the cobbles.

'No,' said Plaintly, 'that was too soon. Le Groutt, come here. Barunko, let Le Groutt take your wrist, yes, like that. He's going to lead you to the wall. When you get there, you throw him, upward. Straight up. Got it?'

'Got it. Show me the wall. Where's Le Groutt?'

'He's holding your wrist,' said Plaintly. 'Now, Le Groutt, lead him out there and quick about it.'

Lurma moved up alongside her and they watched Le Groutt pull Barunko towards the wall, close to Mortari's motionless form. 'Plaintly?'

'What?'

'I'm going to scout to the left there. Think I see something.'

'Go ahead, just be stealthy.'

She scowled above her crossed eyes. 'Don't patronize me, Plaintly.'

Shrugging, mostly to herself as she watched Lurma skitter one way and then that across the street, Plaintly returned her attention to Le Groutt and Barunko.

Symondenalian crept to her side, working his knife around one hand. 'More than Barunko's sight is dull,' he opined.

Plaintly Grasp turned on him. 'That's what I always hated about you, Symon. You're so judgemental.'

'What? That man made a habit of using his head to bash in doors!'

'And there wasn't a door that his head couldn't bash in!'

At the wall, Le Groutt had positioned Barunko beneath one of the spikes, in the dried puddle of all that had leaked out from the corpse speared on it, and was whispering in the man's ear. Nodding, Barunko grasped hold of Le Groutt, and in one swift surge, flung the man upward.

Le Groutt sailed up past the spike, scrabbled desperately at the wall, and then slid back down. The spike impaled his left thigh, arresting his fall. He dangled there for a moment, and then began writhing alongside the withered corpse.

'Come on,' hissed Plaintly and she and Symon hurried across to join Barunko.

Their muscle was crouched in a combative pose. 'Did I do it?' he asked when Plaintly and Symon arrived. 'I heard a whimper! Is he hanging on?'

'Oh,' said Symon, 'he is at that, Barunko.'

There was a groan from Mortari, and a moment later the man slowly sat up, one side of his head so swollen it seemed another head was trying to make its way out from his cheek and temple.

'What's leaking on me?' Barunko asked.

'That'd be Le Groutt,' said Symon. Then he dropped his

knife. It landed point first on his right foot, sliding neatly through the leather of his shoe, slicing through everything else until it jammed in the sole. Symon stared down at the quivering weapon. 'Fuck,' he said, 'that hurts.'

'Stop pissing about, Symon,' hissed Plaintly. 'Barunko, that was a good throw. Honest. He just got hung up on the spike.' She squinted upward. 'Looks like he's trying to pull himself loose.'

Mortari used the wall to stand up. 'There were puppies,' he said. 'I never thought she'd have puppies. I should've guessed, the way she kept coming back and hanging around.'

Lurma Spilibus joined them. 'I found an old postern gate,' she said. 'Picked the lock. We're in.'

'Great work,' Plaintly said, and then turned back to Barunko. 'Barunko, you got to throw Mortari up there, so he can help get Le Groutt off that spike.'

'Throw Mortari,' Barunko said, nodding.

Plaintly pushed Mortari into Barunko's huge hands. 'Here he is—'

Barunko threw the man upward.

There was a thud, a scrape, and then a yelp.

Plaintly stepped slightly away from the wall and looked up. She placed her hands on her hips, and then said. 'Okay, good throw. Symon, get that knife out of your foot, you're next.'

Ambassador Ophal D'Neeth Flatroq exited the compound via the back postern gate, creeping out into the alley. It was dark. Just how he liked it. Hunched in his black snake-skin cloak he peered up and then down the alley. A scrawny cat eyed him from a heap of rubbish, hackles slowly lifting. Meeting its lambent eyes, Ophal's tongue darted out and he blinked.

The cat fled in a scatter of dried leaves and pod husks.

Ophal crept deeper into the shadows, edging along a wall, his broad, bare, nail-less feet silent on the grimy cobbles. There was a route to the Royal Palace that never left alleys and unlit stretches of street. He had made use of it many times in the decade or so of his posting in the city of Farrog. Ideally, he would meet no-one en route, but that was no certainty. Encounters were unfortunate, but he had long since grown used to inspiring terror in the natives, and without question some advantages accrued with the reputation now attending the lone Ambassador of Nightmaria.

His was the only embassy in existence, a concession to the proximity of Farrog to the High Kingdom. As a general rule, his people avoided contact with neighboring realms. To be sure, familiarity was the seed of contempt, and history was replete with welcoming kingdoms suffering the eventual ignominy of cultural degradation, moral confusion and the eventual, and fatal, loss of self-identity.

All trade was strictly prescribed. No foreigner had ever managed to penetrate the kingdom beyond the trade posts situated along the borders at one of the seven high-roads. The lands to either side of the high-roads were a maze of gorges, sheer cliffs, sink-holes and crevices, and even there, watchful wardens ensured that no hardy adventurer or spy ever managed to slip into the high plateaus where the cities of the Imperial Kingdom thrived in their splendid isolation.

How he missed his home! And yet, necessities abided, responsibilities settled their burden, and besides, no-one back there much liked him, anyway.

Sighing, he continued on, creeping from alley to shadow, narrow wend to the twisted and foul trenches of the city's open sewers, his only company thus far resident rats, kilaptra worms, and three-eyed dart-snakes. Of these, he made an effort to avoid only the dart-snakes, as they were in the habit of trying to nest in whatever cracks and folds of the flesh a body might possess. For all his . . . eccentricities, Ophal was relieved that obesity did not count among them. Come to think of it, he could not recall the last time he'd seen an over-weight citizen of Farrog. Mostly, from what he could discern from the high narrow windows of the embassy tower, the swarming figures below all shared a wretched hint of emacia-tion. It was, therefore, a mystery where the dart-snakes nested.

The question remained with him, gnawing away inside. An examination of the matter seemed worthy of some diligence, pointing at some treatise or at least a monograph. Assuming he'd find the time, and all things considered, the next while promised to be somewhat busy.

This new, belligerent and entirely unreasonable king of Far-rog had made all too plain his venal desires, and now his wish would be answered. The Ambassador of Nightmaria was this night on his way to the Royal Palace, to deliver the official dec-laration of war between Nightmaria and Farrog.

His exploration of the nesting habits of three-eyed dart-snakes would, alas, have to wait.

As he made his way along a walled trench, ankle-deep in foul sewage, a kitten appeared on the ledge to his left, scam-pering along the narrow track. His hand snapped out, knobby, scaled fingers closing tight about the creature. It squealed, but the cry was short-lived, as he quickly broke its neck and then, disarticulating his lower jaw, began pushing the mangled furry carcass into his mouth.

In his wake but at a safe distance, a veritable carpet of dart-snakes slithered after him, enraptured by something like worship.

'Now's the time,' hissed Plaintly Grasp, glaring across at Lurma Spilibus, who scowled back at her.

They were all huddled against the wall, the gaping postern entranceway close by. Blood smeared the cobbles beneath Mortari and Le Groutt, while Symondenalian Niksos
had pulled off his thin leather moccasin to tip it upside down
so that it could drain. Barunko had just punched at his own
shadow, thinking it was a guard, cracking two knuckles against
the wall.

'But we're not even inside yet!' retorted Lurma.

'Getting in's always the hardest part,' Plaintly replied. 'Now
we've done that and healing's needed. Le Groutt can't walk
and Mortari's . . . well, Mortari's not all here.'

'Not one of them looked like me,' Mortari said, his swollen head tilted to one side. 'No matter what anybody said.' His
tongue edged up to lick at the fluids draining from his nose.
'Besides, I'd been drinking all week and she had the cutest ears.'

'Lurma, get out that unguent, now.'

Snarling, Lurma, known to many as The Fingers, fumbled
in her purse and then withdrew a gilded vial. 'It's my only one,'
she said. 'For when things get really nasty. And now we're about
to sneak into a Royal Palace crawling with demons and who
knows what else. I'm telling you, Plaintly, this is a bad idea.'

'Hand it over.'

Lower lip trembling, Lurma passed the vial over. She and
Plaintly struggled for a moment getting their hands to meet,
as Lurma kept snatching the vial to the sides. 'Just take it already!'

'I'm trying! Hold still!'

Finally, with the vial in hand, Plaintly crouched beside Le
Groutt. 'Here,' she said, 'one mouthful's all you need. This is
potent stuff.'

Lurma snorted. 'Of course it is. Only the best for The Fingers. And now it's being wasted.'

'He's got a hole through his leg, Lurma,' said Plaintly, 'big enough for you to run your arm through.'

'I've seen worse,' Lurma replied, crossing her arms. 'I could run half a day with a scratch like that.'

Le Groutt gulped down his mouthful, and then settled back, sighing.

Turning to Mortari, Plaintly said, 'Now you, Mortari.'

'She howled outside my window for I don't know how many nights.'

'I bet she did. Here, drink. One swallow!'

Mortari drank down a mouthful and handed the vial back. 'A spike went through my shoulder,' he said. 'Not good.' He frowned. 'And my head. What's wrong with my head? Ma always said to let sleeping dogs lie, but did I listen? I must have. The puppies didn't look like me at all, not a chance.'

Le Groutt grunted. 'Healed the flesh wounds, but his brain's still addled.'

'It's not so bad,' said Mortari, blinking, 'being addled. She had this manic look afterwards, eyes all wild. Gave me the shivers. That's just how it is, all those regrets after you went and did it. Anyway, after dropping the puppies she just let herself go, you know what I mean? Udders dragging and all that. I was still young. I had a future!'

Plaintly handed the vial back to Lurma. 'See?' she said, 'there's some left.'

'Hey,' hissed Symon The Knife, 'what about me?'

'Not enough blood came out of that moccasin,' said Plaintly. 'You'll manage.'

'But I'm a knife fighter! I need to be light on my feet, dancing this way and that, dipping and sliding and weaving, a blur of deadly motion, blades flashing and flickering in the moonlight—'

'Just throw the fucking things and run,' muttered Lurma. 'It's what you always do.'

Symon twisted round to her. 'What's that supposed to mean?'

Plaintly Grasp, known to many as The Fence, held up her hands. 'Stop bickering, you two! Le Groutt, you up to taking point?'

'Point, aye. I got eyes like a cat. Handholds. Footholds.' He pulled from his bag a coil of rope. Seeing Plaintly's frown, he said, 'Might be traps.'

'Traps? This ain't some Jhagut sepulcher, Le Groutt. It's a fucking palace.'

Le Groutt's face turned stubborn. 'I don't go nowhere without my rope. And my ball o'wax. And my Cloak of Blending—'

'Your what?' Symon asked with a snicker. 'Oh, you mean that dusty poncho, right, sorry.'

'Dust, aye,' Le Groutt said in a half-snarl. 'To blend me into the walls and whatnot.'

'Just get going,' Plaintly said. 'Then you, Symon, followed by Mortari and then Lurma and then me. Barunko takes up the rear.'

'Up the rear,' said Barunko, 'Let me at 'im!'

Etched pentagrams of various sizes crowded the floor, with only a narrow path winding amongst them. Emancipor stood just inside the doorway, licking lips that seemed impossibly dry with a tongue that was even drier. His breathing was rapid, with shivers running through him, the sweat on his brow cold as ice.

'Mister Reese? Is something wrong?'

The manservant squinted across at Bauchelain, who stood near a long, narrow table crowded with phials, beakers, stoppered urns, small ornate boxes, clay jars, blocks of pigment, brushes and reeds of charcoal. Upon a shelf above this table was a row of raised disks, each one home to a tiny demon. Most of them squatted motionless in the center of their modest prisons, eyes glittering, although a few paced like caged rats. All bore the smudged remnants of brightly colored paint.

'Mister Reese?'

'Huh? Oh, no Master, I'm fine. More or less. Maybe something I ate.'

'Come along, then, and do recall, stay between the circles on the floor. There is a delicate art to conjuration. A mere misstep could prove disastrous. Now,' he clapped his hands, 'we'll begin with the most demanding of charges, the summoning of an Andelainian Highborn Demon, perhaps even one of royal blood. Once we have compelled that worthy servant, we'll add in a few dozen lesser demons, each serving as bait for the voracious appetites of the Indifferent God. Ah, I tell you, Mister Reese, it has been years since I last felt so . . . enlivened.'

'Aye, Master, I see how excited you must be.'

Bauchelain paused, raising a brow. 'Indeed? Am I so obvious, then?'

'Your beard twitched.'

'It did?'

'Once.'

'Very well, I'll allow you the sharp observation. This time. Imperturbability and equanimity are of course virtues I hold dear, as befits a Master of Necromancy and Conjuration, not to mention a tyrant king—oh no, I shall not be of the frothing variety of the latter, whose antics I find utterly distasteful and, well, embarrassing.'

'Aye, Master, gibbering from the throne's bad form, as you say.'

Bauchelain raised one long finger. 'The illusion of control is essential, Mister Reese, at all times. Now, come along. I need you with me for the summoning.'

Emancipor approached. Carefully. 'What am I to do, Master? A demon prince, you said?'

'Yes. Who shall arrive ill of temper, disgruntled and perhaps even enraged.'

'And, uh, me?'

'You will stand . . . here, as close to the edge of the circle as you can manage, without touching it, of course. Come along, don't be shy. Yes, precisely. Now, don't move.'

'Master?'

'Mister Reese?'

'What do I do next?'

'Why, nothing. Now, the demon, upon seeing you, will naturally reach for you, intent on your messy death. Assuming the pentagram possesses no unseen flaws in its pattern, such as, perhaps, a single cat hair lying athwart the outer ring's line, the demon shall fail in grasping you.'

'Cat hair?' Emancipor turned to the other shelf, the one opposite the one bearing all the tiny demons, where a dozen cats were lying in solemn observation, tails twitching.

'Or some such thing,' Bauchelain murmured. 'Very well then—'

'Sir, if a single cat hair can break the circle, er, shouldn't those creatures be banned from this chamber? I mean, it would seem a reasonable precaution.'

'You might think that,' said Bauchelain, with a slight frown at being interrupted. 'There was a previous concern, you see. Mice.'

'Mice?'

'Many mice, Mister Reese. Possessing slithery tails, a common trait among mice specifically and indeed, all rodents. A mouse that happens to find itself within or athwart a pentagram

at the moment of conjuration, will often suffer the fate of possession. In fact, there are one or two mice still at large, somewhere in this chamber, that are in fact demonic.'

'Demonic mice?'

'Yes, alas. Which is why the cats are all up on that high
shelf.'

'Oh.'

'Leaving me confident that no cat hairs mar the line of the
outer circle.'

'Ah, right.'

'I trust my logic satisfies you, Mister Reese. Now, may I begin?
Thank you. Oh, and say or do nothing that might distract me.'

'Master, I'm afraid I might scream.'

'Presumably, you would only be incited to such indelicacy
following the demon's appearance, at which point the crucial
moment of my concentration will have passed, leaving you
free to scream. If you must.'

'I think, maybe, Master, I must.'

Bauchelain sighed. Adding nothing more, he moved to one
side and faced the pentagram, raising both arms. Eyes narrow-
ing to slits, he began muttering and mumbling an incantation.

This went on for some time. Restless, Emancipor shifted
his weight from one foot to the other, and then scratched at
his behind, which had become unaccountably itchy for some
reason. Also, he needed to empty his bladder. All that wine,
he supposed. Now his nose itched. He rubbed and pushed at
it. Something tickled the back of his throat and he cleared it,
which only made it worse, so he barked a cough—

'Mister Reese! If you please!'

'Sorry, Master. I'm trying!'

'Just . . . be still!'

Nodding, Emancipor settled. Or tried to. Instead, that itch
in his bunghole intensified. Grimacing, he pushed his hand

inside his breeches. Pushed with one finger this way and then that way. Now his left ear tingled. He reached up to push the same finger into that ear—

A deafening thunderclap made him jump.

Within the circle, so massive it filled the entire space, a demon twice Emancipor's height had suddenly appeared, standing in a strange crouch as if a moment earlier it had been sitting at a table. Knees momentarily buckling, it almost toppled backward, and then righted itself. Smoke pouring from its hairless blue hide, sparks raining down from its enormous iron torcs on its upper arms, in one hand it held a haunch of dripping meat and in the other a giant gold goblet now sloshing out burgundy wine.

Turning its blunt, broad, hairless head, its eyes flared bright emerald, fixing on Emancipor. 'You little shit—'

At which point, Bauchelain delicately cleared his throat.

The demon twisted round. 'Blast you to the Seven Fires of Kellanved's Maze! *Again?* And right at dinner . . . *again!* With the delicious High Concubine Allgiva sitting opposite me. *Again!* Scented candles, sweet wine, a priest of Dessembrae turning on the spit! *Again! Damn you Bauchelain and damn you again! Aaargh!*'

'Now now, Prince Flail Their Limbs, how am I to know your circumstances in the moment of summoning? You do me a disservice.'

'Oh, I'll disservice you, Conjurer. One of these nights—'

'Your threats are so tiresome, Prince Flail.'

The demon flung down the haunch of priest thigh, where it bounced, rolled and then spat and sizzled as it struck the invisible barrier of the pentagram. The demon then drained the last of his wine and crushed the goblet into a mangled ruin in his huge, taloned hand. 'This had better be good, and I don't mean hunting any fucking mice!'

Bauchelain smiled in seeming recollection. 'A mere lesson in whom between us has command of the situation, one that, I am sure, need not be repeated.'

'Fuck you, Bauchelain. And don't leave me anywhere near that creepy companion of yours—'

'I won't, although you may come across a few of his charges in the crypts below.'

'Fucking undead. How will I know them?'

'No heads.'

The demon subsided slightly, 'Well, that'll help.'

'Prince Flail Their Limbs, the Indifferent God haunts the levels beneath this palace. He has escaped his latest mortal prison and now seeks a new vessel.'

The demon grunted. 'Let him try me. I'll eat the bastard starting with his left little toe and finish him with the right little toe. I'll chew him into pulp so soft a newborn would think it sweet mother's milk. I'll peel his skin—'

'Yes yes, all that and more, I'm sure,' cut in Bauchelain. 'In the meantime, permit me to assemble for you a small army of minions—'

'But none of those ankle-high little shits you like to paint.'

'No, somewhat more impressive servants, I assure you.'

'They got under my clothes,' the Demon Prince continued in a low grumble. 'One of them tried climbing up my butt-hole, for fuck's sake.'

Flinching, Emancipor straightened, and then quickly reached back under his breeches.

Royal Torturer Binfun Son of Binfun played with his food on the plate before him, using the tip of his knife to prod the over-cooked slab of meat this way and that. He poked it with the two-pronged fork, leaning closer to see if any juices bubbled up from the small punctures. Seeing nothing, he sighed and settled back. 'This is very disappointing,' he said to the desiccated head hanging from a hook opposite him. 'Cook does it deliberately, of course. She's singled me out, has it in for me for some reason. Women are a mystery. They hate for no reason, no reason at all.' Well, of course that was not true. She had a reason. Still, in the greater scheme of things, was he not entirely blameless?

He prodded the meat again. 'Nerve endings, Sire, are the source of all pleasure. This is simple fact. Dead flesh knows no joy, no delight, no sultry tickle of attention. It just . . . lies there. And where pleasure is not possible, why, neither is pain. And yet, does not history reveal a most sordid truth? That generation upon generation, we strive for insensitivity, the muffled simulation of death, benumbed, displaced, inured.'

The severed head of the old king said nothing, but then, he wouldn't, would he? He was dead. Indeed, grimly symbolic was the old king, reminding Binfun that death marked a failure of the torturer's art. Not that he'd had any opportunity to torture the old king. The Usurper's sword was very sharp and the cut beneath the old king's head was the cleanest Binfun had ever examined. A single slice—how he wished he'd seen it!

He stabbed the fork into the slab and left it standing there. 'I am losing weight. Unacceptable. Cook should pay me a visit, an invitation innocuous, beneath suspicion. An offering of wine, suitably drugged in her cup. Then, when she awakens gagged and trussed and utterly helpless . . . no no, I mustn't think such thoughts. Bad thoughts, bad imaginings. Fasting is good for me, so say the Purgists in the Herbmongers' Round. The stomach shrinks, impurities gush and spurt—one can tell they're impurities, given the wretched stench wafting up. And the lightheadedness that follows, why, such luminous clarity!'

He saw the reflected flicker of lamp-light in the old king's dull staring eyes, and twisted round in his chair in time to see Shartorial Infelance stride into the chamber carrying an ornately jeweled oil-lamp. He rose quickly. 'Seneschal, good evening!'

'Sir Binfun, how are you this evening?'

The Royal Torturer bowed before responding. 'Milady, I suffer as it seems I must.'

The tall regal woman glanced down at the small table with its pewter plate and its lone slab of gray meat, and then set down the lamp. 'Ah, the Cook again, is it? Remind me to have another word with her.'

Binfun shrugged. 'I fear it will do no good, Milady, but I do appreciate the effort.'

'Well, I see now that I was not stern enough in reproaching her the last time. This vindictiveness is surely beneath her. Perhaps if I suggest that, should matters not improve, I may have a word with the king . . .'

'Oh, please, Milady, do not do that!'

Shartorial's delicate brows arched. 'An empty threat I assure you. It would be madness to invite the attentions of our liege in such matters. If Cook has any wits, however, the mere hint will set her aright.'

Binfun walked over to the severed head and gave it a light push to set it swinging gently back and forth. 'It's all down to a favorite actor of hers,' he admitted, 'that I had the pleasure of torturing. Or so I assume, since matters turned unpleasant immediately thereafter. But what was I to do? I am the Royal Torturer, and I obey my liege's commands!' The confession seemed to lighten his spirits and he luxuriated in the sensation of unadulterated relief.

'Indeed. Which actor was that?'

'Sorponce Egol, he of the Perfect Profile. Well, it was less than perfect when I was done with it, of course. And making him eat his own nose was perhaps excessive, I do admit.'

'Hmm, how long did he last?'

'Well, that's the thing, most curious. Not by a single instrument or exercise on my part did he give up living. Now, knowing how he used to preen, I set up a full-length mirror, exquisitely polished, so that he could regard himself day and night in the bright light of the dozen lanterns I kept lit. I believe that this broke his will to live. Fatal vanity!'

'I suspect you are correct, Binfun, and that was a most insidious torture, by the way.'

Binfun brightened. 'Yes it was, wasn't it? Thank you, Milady! Your observation has blessed me!' He interlaced his hands before him and smiled. 'Now, I imagine you wish to visit, once more, the one who most fascinates you.'

She shot him a look. 'You've not touched his face?'

'Not once, Milady. Indeed, apart from the rack, he is unmarred, as per your wishes.'

'Excellent.'

'Shall I lead you to the secret spy-hole now?'

'In a moment.'

He smiled. 'Of course. Anticipation is the sweetest nectar, is it not?'

'When are you due your report to the king?' she asked him.

His face fell slightly. 'Ah, I have delayed too long as it is, to be honest, in deference to your desires. Alas, Milady, your visits must soon come to an end, and this is truly tragic for all concerned. I must break the lot, in sessions most foul, and see to it that death delivers its soft kiss of release for each and every one of them. So the king commands.'

Shartorial stepped near the table. She picked up his dinner knife where he'd set it down beside the plate, and idly played with it.

Watching her fondling the knife, Binfum felt his loins stir. 'I will grieve,' he said huskily, 'the end of your visits down here, Milady.'

'Binfun, you say the kindest things. I am flattered.'

'I do regret what awaits the one who fascinates you,' he said. 'And I shall keep him until the last, and be uncommonly quick in taking his life. For you I do this, Milady, and not even the king's command will sway me in this.'

'Very sweet of you,' she said, turning about and plunging the dinner knife into his chest.

He staggered back, reaching futilely at the horn handle jutting from his chest, and then fell into his chair, making the wood creak. He gaped up at her and then frowned. 'Wrong side, Milady,' he gasped. 'This will take some time. Under the . . . *cough* . . . under the heart . . . would have been better . . .'

She looked down at him. 'Quick? I think not. Damn Cook and her petty vindictiveness! What use poison if you don't eat the damned shit?'

'I . . . uh, *cough*, nibbled.'

'You are drowning in your own blood.'

He nodded. 'Subtle . . . after a fashion. *Cough cough!* Unable to shout in alarm. *Cough cough cough!* Guards hear nothing and never *cough* come down besides. *Cough cough cough cough!* Clever, Milady. But, alas, not enough pain.'

'I take little pleasure in this.'

'Oh. Too bad.'

He wheezed, shuddered, and then sagged in the chair, head dipping until his chin rested on his sternum. Red bubbles slid down from his mouth for a few moments, and then the flow ceased.

Shartorial stepped closer and pushed a spiked heel down upon his left foot.

'Ow.'

'Fuck, just get it over with!'

'T-tell Cook . . .'

'What? Tell her what?'

'Tell her . . . *cough, gasp!* Next time . . . medium rare.'

'I can't help it if every woman finds me desirable,' Apto Canavalian was saying. 'There's something impish about me, or so I'm told. They fling themselves at me, to be honest. I have to beat them off. Personally, I think it's down to me being a critic, an arbiter of taste, if you will. Such talent demands a high intellect and that becomes pretty obvious, I suppose, even after the briefest of conversations—'

'Gods below,' moaned Brash Phluster, writhing feebly on the rack, 'somebody kill him. Please.'

'I'm just explaining why I got invited to all the soirées and fêtes, and how all those lovely women ended up dangling on my arm. You know, all things considered, it was almost worth it.'

'Tiny will put him on the rack,' said Tiny Chanter. 'Notch him up until he's dangling from everywhere.'

'I've saved up my biggest bribe,' said Apto, smiling across at Tiny. 'Next time the Royal Torturer comes, I'm offering him my villa. To just let me slip away. The rest of you are dead anyway, so it's not like anyone will know, and I'll hightail it out of Farrog that very night. I hear there's a festival looking for judges down the coast, in Prylap.'

'Tiny's got a better bribe,' said Tiny, his small eyes glinting in the gloom. 'Tiny promises not to tear the torturer's head off. Beats a villa, doesn't it, Midge?'

'Beats it clean.'

'Flea?'

'No head tear beats a villa every time,' said Flea.

THE FIENDS OF NIGHTMARIA

'You're in magicked chains, Tiny,' Apto pointed out. 'No shapeshifting crap from you. Your nemesis necromancer's got you all figured out.'

'Torturer has to unchain Tiny to get him on the rack.'

'I'll warn him this time. Besides, he puts that collar on you first, and it's magicked, too.'

'Tiny will bite out his throat when he gets close.'

'Right,' snapped Apto, 'and *then* you'll threaten not to tear his head off, right?'

'Exactly. Tiny's got it figured out.'

Apto looked over to Midge and then Flea. 'And you let this brainless dolt stay in charge? No wonder you're all in chains and about to die. Your sister had it right—run off with the Assassin and fuck you all.'

Tiny strained at his chains, glaring at Apto. 'We don't talk about her!'

'Well, I am! Listen! Relish Chanter is the smartest Chanter of them all! Smart enough to lose all you dead-weight brothers! Relish Relish Relish! She slept with me, you know? Jumped me right here in Farrog, before running off with Flicker. She was wild, an animal of lust! I needed a healer after she was done with me!'

'Lies!' roared Tiny Chanter. 'Lies and lies and more lies!'

Midge was crying, Flea glowering in deadly silence. A sudden shiver took Apto Canavalian and he decided he'd said enough. Maybe too much. He waved a hand, weakly as the shackles were heavy. 'I'm kidding. I was lying. Just teasing you. She never jumped me, and for all I know, the Assassin kidnapped her—'

'Of course he did!' Tiny bellowed.

'Besides,' added Apto, 'I was thinking, a whole damned villa should be enough to get us all out of here.'

At that, Tulgord Vise straightened in his chains. 'That had better not be a tease, Critic,' he said in a growl.

'It's not,' Apto promised. 'I mean, think on it. We all survived the journey here. We even survived the Assassin's treachery. Like it or not, a bond has formed among us all. It's always that way with survivors. We're inextricably linked because of what we all shared and in case you've forgotten, that journey was one long nightmare.'

'It wasn't so bad,' grumbled Tiny.

'Well, for those of us under threat of getting eaten—'

Brash Phluster lifted his head. 'But that wasn't you, was it, Apto the Corrupt Critic from the Squalid Pits of Evil Betrayal? No! It was us artists! Us ones with, with *talent!* No, not you! You cheated your way out of that, too, like the cheater you are!'

'Perhaps,' said Apto, 'but then, we had to suffer your singing, Phluster. And let's face it, even this Royal Torturer's got nothing on that.'

Tiny laughed. 'Hah hah hah!' and then glared at his brothers, who then laughed, too.

'Hahah!'

'Hah! Hah!'

And now sudden lamp-light lit the corridor beyond the barred door.

Apto straightened. 'All right, friends,' he whispered. 'It seems he's early but no matter. This is the moment. Wish me the Lady's Pull of Luck, wish it for all our sakes!'

The light brightened, and then suddenly dimmed as a hooded face appeared in the door's barred window.

Not the Royal Torturer after all. Some instinct told Apto that this was a woman, a beautiful woman who now watched them from the impenetrable shadows of the hood. He managed a bow. 'Milady,' he said in a soft murmur.

'I have been watching you all,' came the sibilant reply.

'Ah,' smiled Apto. 'I admit, on occasion, that I sensed hidden eyes, a certain fixation of attention, vision's lingering caress—'

'I looked upon the one with the broken leg.'

'I'm sorry, what?'

Keys ground in the lock and then the door squealed open.

Steck Marynd had sat up straighter at the back of the cell, an expression of curiosity upon his craggy and singularly unattractive features. Apto looked at the backwoods simpleton and felt a flood of acidic venom.

Dressed in opulent silks, the woman seemed to whisper into the chamber, floating like a dream. She crossed straight over to stand before Steck Marynd. 'Your leg, has it healed, sir?'

'I tend to think so,' he replied, 'until I'm on the rack.'

'Yes, that was most cruel. But no more will the Royal Torturer have his way with you. Indeed, even now his corpse grows cold. I am here, sir, to free you.'

Struggling, Steck regained his feet. 'Milady, that is most kind. Perhaps you could start with the poor man on the rack.'

She seemed to tilt her head. 'I said "you," sir, and I meant just that.'

Steck frowned, and then crossed his arms. 'I'm afraid I must decline your invitation, Milady. These are my companions, after all. Should you unlock my shackles, nothing can prevent me from doing the same to theirs.'

'Ah, I see. Well, why should I be surprised? I could see your innate nobility, and the bright virtue that is your loyalty. Still, your fellow prisoners spoke derisively of you, sir, without pause.'

'Theirs is a gruff camaraderie, Milady.'

'Tiny loves Steck,' said Tiny, and then he scowled. 'Not like that. Tiny loves women, lots of women, more women than Tiny can count. Right Midge?'

'That would be seven women,' said Midge, 'since you can't count past six.'

'Flea loves Steck, too,' said Flea. 'Flea loves Steck more than he loves his brothers. More than he loves women. More even than he loves Relish, his sister. More even—'

'For the love of decency,' said Apto, 'stop now, I beg you.'

Sighing, the woman lifted up the ring of keys. 'Very well, sir, you shall have your wish.'

'Milady, have you planned for us a way out? There are many guards in the level above us.'

'Unaccountably,' she replied, 'none were present.'

Steck frowned. 'None? But—'

At that moment an inhuman scream howled through the corridors, ending in a strangled snarl. Someone then shrieked, and that cry ended much more abruptly.

'Gods,' moaned Brash Phluster, 'what was that?'

With trembling hands, the woman set to Steck's bindings. 'We need to get out of here!'

'Tiny's not afraid,' said Tiny in a thin voice.

'Midge is,' said Midge.

Mute and pale, Flea nodded. 'Afraid. Eek!'

The forgotten postern gate cut through the outer wall of the palace, but doors to the right and the left in the wall itself opened into narrow cavities, with steps going down. As the palace's main gate was to the right, Plaintly Grasp decided that the left passage was likely the one they desired, so down they went, Le Groutt in the lead with a stubby candle in one hand and a coil of rope in the other.

'This just goes round and round the outer wall,' hissed Symondenalian Niksos. 'We should have gone further in, Plaintly, down through the coal cellar, or maybe the courtyard well.'

'I used to swim in my Pa's well,' said Mortari. 'That's how I found all the drowned cats. Those cats must've been the clumsiest cats in the world, and all drowning in a single night like that. I figure one fell in and the others tried to help. Anyway, the worst bit was bumping into them, or getting a mouthful of manky fur. The water tasted of them for weeks, too.'

'Mortari,' whispered Plaintly, 'can you save the tales for some other time? We don't want anyone hearing us.'

'Pa never liked cats. He liked lizards, you see, and the cats kept killing the lizards, or eating their tails, so Pa would beat the cats back and rescue them. The lizards, I mean, even the ones without tails.'

'Symon,' said Plaintly, 'we're not going round and round. We're well under the wall's foundations now. We've been going down forever. This used to be a citadel, remember, the whole damned hilltop. Look! Le Groutt's found us a side passage and it's heading the right way.' She pushed up past Lurma and then Mortari and then Symon The Knife until she could rest a hand on Le Groutt's shoulder. Together, they peered into the narrow crack that led off from the rough staircase.

'Scout it out some,' she said to Le Groutt. 'Twenty paces, then come back.'

'Twenty paces,' he said, nodding. 'That'd be ten paces in, ten paces back, right? Got it.'

'No. Twenty paces in, twenty back.'

'That's forty paces, Plaintly. You said twenty.'

'I meant twenty in. I don't care how many to get back.'

'Well, it'd be twenty, wouldn't it? Unless I only came back halfway, or if I took long jumps. Could be any number then, between one and twenty, I mean. Or baby steps could make it, like, fifty!'

'That's all very true. Good points, Le Groutt. But let's make it as easy as possible. Twenty paces in, see if it goes past that, and then come back and tell us.'

'I won't be able to see if it goes past twenty, Plaintly, unless I go and find out.'

'Okay, stop at twenty and then do ten more. If that ten was the same as the first twenty, then come back.'

'Now we're talking upwards of sixty paces if you count both ways, and then another thirty if we decide to go that way.'

'Your point?'

Le Groutt bared his teeth. 'I get a bigger cut for doing more pacing than any of you.'

'Cut? What cut? We're trying to free the Head of the Thieves' Guild.'

Le Groutt frowned. 'Oh, right.' He then brightened. 'But there's bound to be treasure squirreled away down here, a vault or something! A Royal Vault! We could clean it out once we've sprung the old hag—'

'Old hag? That's Mistress Dam Loudly Heer you're talking about!'

'She doesn't like me,' said Le Groutt. 'I only came for the loot.'

'There won't be any loot!'

'And you still expect me to walk an extra nine hundred paces?'

'Nine hundred? What are you talking about? Just scout the damned passage!'

'I'm a 2nd story man, Plaintly, not a scout.'

'So you won't do it?'

Le Groutt crossed his arms. 'No. I won't.'

Sighing, Plaintly turned and took Symon by the arm. 'You, take that candle and scout this passage.'

'Ten percent extra on my cut.'

'Fine! Now go!'

Symon snaked past Le Groutt, reached back to snag the candle, and then set off.

'That's not fair!' hissed Le Groutt, 'I was only gonna ask for five percent!'

'That's what you get for arguing,' said Plaintly. 'Now The Knife gets ten percent of your cut.'

'*What?*'

'Shhh!'

'Ever had lizard tail soup?' Mortari asked. 'Ma used to make the best lizard tail soup. Boiled up in cat water. Even Pa couldn't complain.'

After some scrabbling sounds, and then a low yelp, the faint candle-light from the passage winked out.

Plaintly held up a hand when Le Groutt was about to speak. She listened, and then shook her head. 'That's not good. I don't hear anything.'

'Of course you don't,' said Le Groutt, 'you told me to shut up.'

'Not you,' she said. 'Symon.'

'Where is he?'

'He went down this passageway, remember?'

'It was a well,' Mortari said behind them. 'Full of drowned cats, floating and bobbing and smelling bad. That's when I found Granma.'

'I don't see any passageway,' said Le Groutt.

'Light another candle,' said Plaintly.

Le Groutt fidgeted in his bag for a few moments, and then he said, 'I only brought the one.'

Plaintly twisted round. 'Anyone else bring a candle?'

'I knew Le Groutt had one,' said Lurma.

'We only had the one candle?' Plaintly asked.

'I had one,' said Barunko. 'Then I took it in my hand and crushed it like it was melted wax. Ha!'

'Where is it now, Barunko?' Plaintly asked.

A moment of silence, and then Barunko said, 'I don't remember. It was years ago.'

'Le Groutt,' said Plaintly, 'you're going to have to creep along in the dark. You need to find Symon and that candle.'

'Where?'

'Down this passageway.'

'Here,' said Le Groutt, 'take this end of the rope.'

Plaintly took it and handed it to Mortari, who moved up to lean close to Le Groutt. They whispered back and forth for a bit and then with a grunt Le Groutt clambered into the passageway.

A short time later there was a cry, the sound of falling rocks, and then silence.

Plaintly sighed. 'Mortari, give me the end to that rope.'

Mortari held up both hands. 'Which one?'

'What? He gave you the other end, too?'

'Just to make sure, he said,' explained Mortari.

'Lurma,' said Plaintly, 'you've got the sensitive touch. Get down this passage, feel your way, and be careful!'

'Should've sent me to start with,' said Lurma. 'I was offering four percent. Not that anyone bothered asking me. No, it's just "pick that lock, Lurma!" and "Listen at that door, Lurma!" and "Lift that key ring from his belt, Lurma!"'

'Okay okay,' said Plaintly, 'sorry.'

She wriggled past and then slipped into the crack in the wall. They waited.

'She gave me the clap, too,' said Mortari. 'The bitch.'

'Who?' asked Barunko.

'I told you. The bitch.'

'But who?' Barunko demanded.

'I told you!'

'No you didn't!'

'Be quiet, both of you! I hear something!' Plaintly edged

into the passageway. 'Voices. Faint. Wait, I can almost make them out.'

'What are they saying?' Mortari asked.

'They're arguing . . . about . . . about, uh, who's got the end of the rope. Wait! Symon's found the candle! Come on you two, let's go. They've found a genuine tunnel!'

'A tunnel!' exclaimed Barunko. 'Here? Underground?'

'Plaintly?' asked Mortari.

'What?'

'What should I do with these rope ends?'

'How many have you got?'

'Two.'

'Bring 'em,' she said. 'Might come in handy.'

The passageway was narrow, the footing treacherous, but the sudden flare of candle-light ahead helped them reach the others. There was a ledge and then a drop of perhaps half a man's height, and sitting on the floor of the tunnel below were Symon, Le Groutt and Lurma.

Plaintly clambered over the ledge and dropped down, Mortari and Barunko following.

The tunnel was wide, low-ceilinged, the ceiling being the narrow top of converging planes of set stone blocks. Brightly painted friezes covered the walls to either side, and the floor was made of shiny marble tiles. Plaintly took the candle from Symon and brought the light close to one of the paintings. 'I don't recognize any of this—must be thousands of years old— no, wait, is that the new king?' She brushed a finger against the frieze. 'Paint's still wet!'

Barunko sniffed. 'I smell shit.'

Lurma rolled one of her eyes. 'The word is "shitty," Barunko.'

'No,' said Symon The Knife, 'he's right! It's coming from down this way.' And he set off down the tunnel.

'We're tracking shit smells now?' Lurma asked.

Symon had disappeared behind a bend and now they heard his low cry. Plaintly in the lead, they hurried over.

Two bodies were lying on the floor at Symon's feet.

'Fast work, Symon!' said Lurma around her wad of Prazzn. 'Those painters couldn't paint worth crap!'

The Knife spun round. 'Wasn't me! Look at them! They've been torn apart!'

'Besides,' said Plaintly, 'if you'd bothered looking as carefully as I did, you'd have seen that the painters were just painting over some ancient king, replacing it with the Usurper's face. Desecrating historical artifacts! Skewing the timeline for generations of historians to come! I told you he was evil!'

'Skewing the what?' Symon asked as he drew his knife. 'Listen! Some wild beast is prowling these tunnels. Look at that smear of shit there—it's still fresh! We're not alone, is what I'm saying.'

'Symon's right,' said Le Groutt. 'There's me and Mortari and Plaintly and Lurma and—'

Lurma took a swing at Le Groutt's head and missed. 'He means there's a fucking demon down here is what he means, Le Groutt!'

'A demon! Where?'

'Close,' hissed Symon, tossing his knife from one hand to the next. A moment later it clattered to the floor.

Everyone tensed but thankfully, the skidding knife missed the smear of shit.

Sighing, Plaintly said, 'Pick that up, Symon, you might need it. I want you on point—'

'Me? Why not Barunko?'

'Yes,' said Barunko, 'why not Barunko, and where is he, anyway?'

'He's right here,' said Plaintly. 'You're Barunko, Barunko.'

'That's right! I'll take point! Where's point?'

Plaintly pushed him forward. 'We go this way,' she said.

'Why that way?' Symon demanded.

Plaintly grasped Barunko and spun him round. 'All right, we go that way!'

'That's better,' grunted Symon. 'Unless the other way's better.'

'It isn't,' snapped Plaintly. 'We're looking for the crypts.'

'So how do you know the crypts are that way?' demanded Symon, wiping blood from his hands.

'I don't.'

They set out, Barunko in the lead, his hands held out to make sure he didn't walk into a wall. Behind him, Lurma carried the candle and weaved from one side of the tunnel to the other and then back again, as was her wont. Behind her, Mortari walked with his swollen head tilted to one side, the strange bulges resting on his left shoulder. On his heels was Le Groutt, rope coiled in one hand. Then came Plaintly with Symon The Knife right behind her.

'Keep an eye out behind us,' Plaintly whispered to Symon.

'I'm trying,' he replied, 'only, it's dark back there, and I swear, that darkness is following us! Like some creeping tide of doom!'

'Just be ready in case something jumps us. Where's your other knife, anyway? I haven't seen it.'

'I lost it. Last week.'

'Oh, too bad. How'd you lose it?'

'It got stuck through the ear of a mule and the mule ran off.'

'You tried to assassinate a mule?'

'It seemed an easy twenty Broaches. That was one stubborn mule and the farmer was fed up having to carry all the bundles to market every day.'

'The bundles weren't on the mule's back?'

'Like I said, it was stubborn, and cranky.'

'So why did the farmer keep dragging the mule back and forth to market if it wasn't carrying anything?'

Symon snorted. 'I didn't say he was a smart farmer, did I? Twenty Broaches!'

'But you failed.'

'He paid me anyway, for the lost knife.'

Plaintly smiled and nodded. 'Clever, Symon. Seems you've learned from me after all and it only took how many years?'

'Not really. That knife was worth fifty.'

'Better twenty Broaches back than a kick in the head, though.'

'Well, it was the kick that messed up my aim.'

'Oh.'

Le Groutt twisted round to glare at them. 'Are you two done?'

'We're just passing the time,' hissed Symon The Knife. 'What's your problem, Le Groutt?'

'You getting ten percent of my take! That's my problem!'

Up ahead there was a loud thump. Barunko had run into a door. Everyone clumped up behind him while he searched for the latch. After a few moments of this, Lurma snarled and pushed past the Muscle. 'Here, let me.' After a few tries, she clasped hold of the latch, turned it, opened the door, and glanced back triumphantly at Plaintly.

But no-one was really paying her any attention, for on the other side of the doorway crouched an ape-like demon with both hands savagely working its engorged penis. Glancing up, it blinked and then smiled, revealing a row of sharp fangs.

Symon's knife hissed through the air, but from long experience everyone had already ducked, even Barunko. The weapon flew past the demon to land far down the corridor.

Ignoring the demon, whose rocking had not abated, Mortari bolted after it.

'Attack, Barunko!' cried Plaintly. 'Straight ahead! Attack!'

As Barunko surged forward, the demon shuddered and then spurted all over the huge man. Who reeled back. 'Aagh! My eyes!'

Squealing, the demon rushed off down the corridor, barreling over Mortari who had retrieved the knife with a wild, excited grin. He leapt back to his feet and scurried towards Symon. 'I got it!' he cried. 'Throw it again!'

Plaintly snapped, 'Forget all that! Lurma, help get Barunko cleaned up, will you?'

'What? Have you lost your mind?'

'Just use that flask of water and at least rinse out his eyes.'

'What if I get pregnant?'

'That would only happen,' Plaintly explained, 'if you wiped down his face with your crotch.'

'Crotch!' said Barunko, groping wildly. 'Face! Hurry!'

Scowling, Lurma drew out the flask. 'This was my special water,' she said.

'Why?' Plainty asked. 'What's special about it?'

'It's the flask I drink from,' Lurma replied. 'Now I'm wasting it, on Barunko's face. I hope everyone's paying attention, because I'll be wanting compensation for everything I'm using up here.'

'I hope you get pregnant,' said Le Groutt.

'What?'

'You'd look pretty with that special glow.'

'Fuck off, Le Groutt.'

'Hey! I was complimenting you! Hood's breath, you're a sour one, aren't you? That's what happens when you ain't got that glow.'

Plaintly said, 'Just hurry up, will you? We've got to keep moving. It's not like we've got all night, is it?'

Symon frowned at her. 'Yes it is,' he said. 'We've got all night. What are you going on about, Plaintly?'

'Oh, just hurry,' she said, rubbing wearily at her face.

'You have a very wet crotch,' Barunko observed after Lurma sprayed his eyes with the flask. 'Are you peeing? You should have told me. I would've opened my mouth.'

In his years in the diplomatic service of Nightmaria, such as it was, Ophal D'Neeth Flatroq had become a man with far too much time on his hands, leading him to a more or less ongoing contemplation on the nature of political power in the modern age. He was not yet prepared to set forth anything like a theorem, since he remained in the stage of assembling a lengthy list of observations, characteristics and other such details as required prior to formulating any particular set of rules and such.

One obstacle to this process was a dearth of experience, since his only contact with such rulers amounted to the previous—now dead—King N'Gorm (the Lesser), and now the usurper, Bauchelain the First. Still, of histories there were plenty available in Farrog's Grand Library of the Arts, Alchemy, Nature and Divination, a small building off Harbor Square consisting of an imposing Archivist's Desk forming a barrier between the public and the collection, the latter of which consisted of twelve bound books, eighteen scrolls and seven stone tablets. As formidable as the desk was, it was the Archivist who naturally posed the greatest obstacle to perusing the Royal Collection of Letters. Fortunately, the poor man possessed a neurotic terror of snakes, lizards, toads and frogs: creatures either slimy or scaly or both, a descriptive that one could, without stretching, reasonably apply to Ophal himself.

In any case, certain arrangements had been reached between the Ambassador and the Archivist, permitting Ophal's access to the collection in the span of time between the midnight bell and dawn. As it turned out, the accumulated wisdom of the Farrogese had proved most illuminating, if somewhat depressingly limited.

Prior to King N'Gorm there had been a succession of mostly ineffectual rulers in Farrog. If this seemed a cruel assessment, it was nothing compared to Ophal's opinion of N'Gorm himself. In a cool and clinical state of mind, one might assert that the man had been excruciatingly useless, and indeed, that his ignominious assassination was in fact a mercy for all concerned (arguably including N'Gorm himself).

That said, as Ophal sat in the waiting room outside the Throne Room, the rule of King N'Gorm served a useful counterweight in Ophal's potential polemic concerning the art of political leadership, with the other end of the spectrum occupied by King Bauchelain the First.

Politically and under the present circumstances, of course, Ophal would rather N'Gorm had kept both his head and his throne, thus obviating the need for this fateful meeting.

Hearing a faint scuff from the doorway, Ophal glanced up and flinched back upon finding the Grand Bishop Korbal Broach standing there, small flat eyes fixed upon the Ambassador.

Clearing his throat, Ophal nodded in greeting. 'Prrlll ffllap—'

'Stop that,' said Korbal Broach.

'Ethcuse me, good ewening, Gwand Bithop.'

'I have proclaimed a holy war, Ambassador.'

'Yeth, why?'

Korbal Broach frowned. 'Because . . . I felt like it?'

'Aahh.'

The Grand Bishop stared down at him for a while longer.

Ophal fidgeted.

'I don't worship any gods,' Korbal Broach then said.

'Not ewen the . . . prrlll . . . Indifferent God?'

'Oh no. In fact, we're trying to kill him. He's hard to kill.'

'Yeth, I'm thure.'

'He's obsessed with sex.'

'Prrlll. Awen't we all?'

Korbal Broach blinked. 'No.'

All things considered, it was probably a requirement among all tyrants to possess a companion such as this Korbal Broach; indeed, Ophal was nearing the formulation of a truism regarding insanity as a prerequisite to tyranny. The absence of conscience, the curious shallowness of contemplation, a cool pragmatism leading to the justification of all manner of depravity, slaughter and inhumanity. Such individuals were clearly useful for the tyrant, assuming one appreciated a sounding board throwing back raving madness at every opportunity.

'I killed all my priests,' said the Grand Bishop.

'Aahh, how . . . thowough of you.'

'They talked too much.'

'Mhmm.'

Korbal Broach stared for a moment longer, and then departed.

Ophal allowed himself to relax. The kitten was coming back on him in a succession of furry burps. It had probably been infected with worms or something. That was the risk that came with unscheduled snacks, particularly in the alleys of Farrog. He was feeling decidedly queasy.

The King's manservant now appeared in the doorway. 'Ambassador? He'll see you now.'

Ophal rose from his seat. 'Prrlll, fflaapp, ethlenent!'

The old man grunted. 'Easy for you to say.' He hesitated,

and then glanced back over a shoulder, before quickly stepping into the chamber. 'Listen, it's bad luck that you're, uh, lizard people. I mean, it's not your fault or anything, is it? It's just what you are, right? But you know, naming your kingdom Nightmaria, well, maybe that worked for old King N'Gorm, but for my master, well, that's more of an, uh, invitation.'

Ophal nodded excitedly. 'Yeth! I too have weathed this concluthion! Ethlenent! Go on, pweathe!'

'And calling yourselves Fiends, well—'

'Aahh! Prrlll! About that—'

Some noise made the manservant turn to the doorway. 'Oops, time to go, Ambassador. Please follow me—oh, you know the drill. Oh and remember, he likes genuflection, and obsequiousness. Groveling is even better. Abject despair soothes him best of all—I've turned that into an art and, well, never mind. Come along.'

The manservant in the lead, they entered the throne room.

The headless corpse straddled Brash Phluster, both pallid hands slapping the artist across the cheeks, back and forth, back and forth. 'Aaagh!' Brash screamed, 'get it off of me! Please!'

For the moment, however, everyone else was too busy fighting off the dozen or so other headless undead crowding the narrow corridor, barring Apto Canavalian, who had found a niche that had, once upon a time, been home to a statue or some such thing, as he found himself on a raised pedestal. Remaining utterly motionless demanded all his nerve, but it seemed to be working, as the horrid decapitated figures seemed to be ignoring him.

In between his moments of utter terror, he found himself musing on how the damned things saw anything at all. The ways of sorcery and necromancy were indeed a mystery, were they not?

The Chanters were laughing as they waded in, stamping sideways into shins and snapping bones so that the undead monstrosities fell over, to flop about before starting to pull themselves along, resuming their pursuit and most of them, Apto saw, were converging on poor Brash Phluster, who had unfortunately fallen over and was now being swarmed.

Off to one side, Steck Marynd protected Shartorial Infelance, in that usual manly fashion of his. Apto knew it all to be an act. It must be. Selflessness was hardly a survival trait, was it? In fact, it was the very opposite.

'Self interest,' he whispered, trying not to move his lips since statues weren't in the habit of commentary. 'The rational course, first and foremost. Always. Who else matters more than me?'

Tulgord Vise was now dragging bodies off of Brash Phluster, lifting them until they dangled, whereupon he snapped their spines over one thigh, like a man assembling firewood, before flinging them to one side to make a neat, tidy stack.

'A man without an axe, that is,' muttered Apto. 'And given how stupid he is, I doubt it's anything new on him. Firewood? Use an axe. No axe? Get someone else to do it. Someone like Tulgord Vise.' He almost snorted a laugh, coming ever so close to drawing the attention of the nearest headless undead.

Eventually, most of the creatures were little more than sacks of dead meat around broken bones, and Brash Phluster was at last able to scramble free, weeping uncontrollably, his cheeks bright red.

'Why?' he cried. 'Why did they do that?'

Deeming it safe at last, Apto stepped down from the pedestal, stretching to work out the stiffness that came with holding the same pose for so long. 'I recognize some of these bodies,' he said. 'They were judges.'

Brash stared at him, and then his swollen face twisted. 'You think you're funny? You're not. Whose idea was it to use that niche and that pedestal? Whose idea was to pose like a statue? Mine! Then you pulled me off and threw me to the ground!'

Apto shrugged. 'I know a good idea when I see it.'

'As Greatest Artist of the Century I was the better fit on that pedestal!'

'Fame is fleeting, isn't it? Us critics prop you up only to drag you down.'

Steck now limped forward. 'We need to keep moving,' he said. 'There's bound to be more of these things, and then there's the demons. We need weapons.' He turned to Shartorial, whose eyes gleamed in worshipful regard as she looked steadily upon Steck Marynd. 'We need to find the guards' armory, Milady, and the lockers where our weapons are kept. Can you lead us there?'

She nodded.

'Tiny don't need weapons,' said Tiny, raising into view his battered fists. 'Tiny breaks bones. Bones go snap.'

'Crunch,' added Midge.

'Splinter,' said Flea, who then frowned.

'No,' rumbled Tulgord Vise. 'A Mortal Sword needs his sword. Otherwise he's just . . .'

'Mortal?' asked Apto.

'You begin to tire me, Critic,' said Tulgord, glowering. 'I am a Mortal Sword, blessed by a goddess, sworn to vengeance against the Nehemoth.' He made a fist. 'And they are almost within reach! This is our best chance!'

'I agree,' said Steck Marynd. 'The time has come to kill them. To finally rid the world of Bauchelain and Korbal Broach.'

Gesturing, Shartorial said, 'I will take you to your weapons! Come!'

They set off, stepping carefully to avoid all the grasping hands and reaching arms.

'All in all,' said Apto as they hurried down the corridor, 'those undead seemed pretty useless.'

Steck grunted. 'Aye. Distractions. Something else is down here in these crypts. I can feel it. Something truly nasty.'

'We've been hearing screams,' said Apto. 'That suggests that you are right, Steck Marynd, and the sooner all of you are armed the safer I'll—I mean *we'll*—feel.'

'Tiny feels safe,' said Tiny. 'Midge?'

'Safe,' said Midge.

'Flea?'

'Splinter,' said Flea. 'Bones go *splinter!* Like that, the sound. They go. The bones. Hah!'

Brash Phluster turned a glare on Apto. 'I'm putting you in my next epic poem. Where you're going to die most horribly, maybe more than once!'

'As a discerning scholar of art, Brash, I already die a thousand deaths with every song you sing, every tale you concoct, every mangled travesty of language you presume to call a poem.'

Brash made a fist, his puffy face working soundlessly, as he struggled through his fury to find words. In the end, he simply shook his fist in Apto's face.

'Oh dear,' said Apto. 'The artist waiting for inspiration . . . wake me when you're ready, won't you?'

Tulgord Vise glanced back at them. 'Stop baiting the poor poet, Critic.'

'He just threatened to impugn my name and reputation!'

'No he didn't. Nobody's heard of you anyway.'

'I have a livelihood to protect!'

Tiny laughed his nasty laugh. 'Deadlihood, soon, if you don't shut your mouth.'

'Mouth,' said Midge.

'Bones,' said Flea.

'I will write an epic poem about all of you,' said Brash Phluster. 'The Nehemothanai, and their trek across half the world, hunting down the evil necromancers Bauchelain and Korbal Broach, slaying them at last in the cursed City of Farrog! I envisage at least twenty thousand stanzas—'

'As prologue, surely,' suggested Apto Canavalian.

Ignoring him, Brash continued. 'Every hero needs a poet, someone who witnesses them being, uh, heroes, and who can sing about them and make them famous, so their names journey down through the centuries.'

'Tiny needs no poet. Tiny journeys down the centuries himself.'

'That doesn't matter,' insisted Brash Phluster. 'Everything you do I'll make bigger, more amazing, more everything.'

'Everything Tiny does is already bigger and more amazing. Like when Tiny takes poet by the neck and twists off his head.'

'Now that's worth a poem all right,' said Apto.

'And then makes critic eat poet's head, so he chokes on poet's words, and hair.'

'You know, Tiny,' Apto observed, 'that quip would work much better with a little work. Might I suggest you delete the "hair" bit?'

'Tiny delete critic.'

'Hair,' said Flea.

Shartorial and Steck arrived at a narrow set of stairs leading upward, where they paused and Steck held up a hand. 'There's blood on these steps,' he whispered. 'Best you all be quiet now.'

'Tiny don't take orders from nobody.'

'Nobody,' agreed Midge.

Rubbing at his face, Steck said, 'Listen, it's just proper caution here. Remember, once we get our weapons, we become formidable and dangerous again, and we can carve our way up into the palace.'

'Tiny's not scared of anything.'

'Fine then,' growled Steck. 'Take the lead here, won't you?'

'You don't order Tiny. Tiny orders you, and you, and you, and you and you.' He pushed past Steck and Shartorial. 'Tiny goes first. You all follow and keep your mouths shut or Tiny shuts them for you, permanently if not forever.'

'You truly are obnoxious,' observed Tulgord Vise.

'That's right. Tiny kills ox with one hand, all the time. Tiny was an oxnobian before any of you were even born, or had mothers and shit.'

'Tiny pulled the legs off a mule when he was six,' said Midge.

'We're wasting too much time,' hissed Shartorial.

Tiny blew her a kiss that sprayed her face with spittle, earning a warning growl from Steck Marynd, but Tiny was already on the stairs and Shartorial reached out a hand to hold Steck back, while using her other hand to wipe at her face.

'Milady,' Apto heard Steck whisper, 'for that insult he'll die. This I swear.'

'It is no matter,' she replied. 'But do kill him at first opportunity anyway.'

'I shall.'

Apto glanced over at Midge and Flea. They stared back stonily. Apto smiled and waved.

Flea smiled and waved back.

Steck then took his new woman by one hand and led her up the stairs in Tiny's wake. Apto shoved Brash to one side to fall in directly behind Shartorial. Cursing, Brash scratched Apto's left ear, only to stumble and bark his shin on the first step. Midge then stepped on the artist, and Flea followed.

Tulgord Vise stopped to drag Brash to his feet. 'Stop being so clumsy, poet.'

'Don't let them kill me,' whimpered Brash.

The Mortal Sword said, 'Fear not, while I live. After all, a world without poets, sir, would be . . . would be . . . er, far less clumsy.'

'But—'

'Get moving and start acting like a man or I'll kill you myself.'

'You're all awful,' Brash Phluster hissed as he clambered his way up the steps. 'My epic poem won't lie about any of you! By the time I'm done with *The Nehemothenai*, the audience will be cheering for the fucking necromancers!'

Hearing that, Apto twisted round, 'Now you're talking!'

Lurma Spilibus gently turned the latch and edged open the heavy door. A ribbon of light cut into the corridor, making everyone tense. She squeezed one eye into the crack, and then leaned back again, rubbing at that eye.

Plaintly whispered, 'What did you see?'

'A very narrow guard room. I couldn't see the walls but what I saw was empty. Except for the bits of flesh and bone and hair and ripped up clothing.'

'Anyone see you?' Le Groutt asked.

'No,' said Lurma, 'I just told you.'

Plaintly nodded. 'Bits of flesh and bone and hair and ripped up clothing.'

'That's what I said, isn't it? Bits of—'

'That must've been some party,' said Symon The Knife.

'Granma's wake was a damned good party,' said Mortari, 'even though she was just missing, but it'd been weeks and nobody takes that long drawing water from the well at the back of the yard. So we decided she was dead, and that was fair, wasn't it? And then, months later, I bumped right into her. In the well, I mean, with all those cats with their tails all tied together.'

Gesturing, Plaintly said, 'Go on, Lurma, check it out.'

But Lurma hesitated. 'Could be traps.'

'What kind of traps?'

'If I knew that they wouldn't be much good as traps, would they? No, leave this to me. Everyone else stay here, and be quiet while I check it out.'

'Good idea,' said Plaintly.

They remained crouched in the corridor, as Lurma Spilibus pushed the door open a bit more, and then slipped sideways into the guard room. A moment later her head popped back into view. 'It's wider than it was before, the room.'

'Anything else?' Plaintly asked.

'Wait.' The head popped out of sight again, and then they heard, 'Two doors in the opposite wall, identical, both ajar.'

'Room for all of us in there?' Plaintly asked.

A hand appeared and waved them in.

They quickly entered the guard room, and then stood around, amidst a knocked over wooden table, shattered chairs, broken plates, dented tankards, bent knives and snapped swords, and an abattoir's worth of chopped up meat and bone along with clumps of shredded, sodden clothing. Six crushed heads were piled up against a wall, along with twelve or so severed feet still wearing an assortment of cheap footwear.

Symon drew his knife. 'Should I check for survivors?' he asked.

'No,' said Plaintly, 'I think it's too late for any of these ones.'

'What do you think happened?' Le Groutt asked, his eyes slightly wild.

'That demon,' said Plaintly.

'The squirting one?' Symon then shook his head. 'Not a chance. That thing ran from us. It wasn't much taller than Mortari here.'

'Assuming I'm Mortari,' said Mortari.

'Well, who else would you be?'

'I don't know. It's a mystery.'

'Lurma,' said Barunko, 'more pee, please.'

'Listen,' said Plaintly, raising a hand to draw everyone's attention, 'something's wrong here.'

'What do you mean?' asked Le Groutt.

'Well, there was that demon, and now this room full of guards who've been torn to bits. It doesn't feel right. You all know to trust my instincts, and I'm saying . . .' she shook her head, 'the sooner we find the Head of the Thieves Guild and get out of here, the better.'

'So where do you think she is?' Lurma asked. 'Plaintly?'

'Plaintly's right here,' said Le Groutt. 'I'm looking at her, in fact.'

'Lurma meant our Mistress,' explained Plaintly, 'and I'm thinking in the cells down the hall, through that door there.'

'Which one?' Lurma asked.

'There's only one,' Plaintly said.

'What? I saw—oh, look at that! Only one door! The other one's vanished! I told you there were traps in here!'

'What kind of trap is a disappearing door?' Symon demanded.

'The kind that makes you go through the other one, of course. You'd better let me check it out first.'

'Symon,' said Mortari, 'let me borrow your knife.'

'What? Now?'

'Just for a moment, I promise.'

Symon handed over his knife. Mortari took it and popped the massive bulbous swelling projecting out from his temple.

A stream of pink goo gushed out. 'Ah,' he said. 'That's better.' He handed the knife back, and then smiled his thanks at Symon.

A slimy puddle was fast forming on the floor at Mortari's feet.

Lurma stared down at it. 'You're going to clean that up, aren't you, Mortari?'

'Of course I am! On our way back, though. Anyone got a handkerchief we can throw over it in the meantime? Don't want any cat drowning in it or anything.'

'You're still leaking everywhere!' said Lurma. 'It's disgusting!'

'Everybody's squirted but me,' said Barunko, his lower lip trembling.

Plaintly moved close to The Muscle. 'It's all right, Barunko. You'll get your turn.'

'Really?'

'I promise,' said Plaintly, who then turned back to Lurma and gestured her towards the door.

Nodding, Lurma edged closer. She approached the door from one side, and then darted across to come at it from the other side. She reached the wall beside it and fumbled at the gore-spattered stones for a moment, before her fingers brushed the edge of the door and then she grasped it and pushed it open. Glanced through and then back. 'A corridor,' she whispered. 'Cell doors on both sides, all broken open.'

'And the other end?' Plaintly asked.

Lurma looked again. 'Two more doors.'

'Two?'

She looked back. 'One.'

'Just one? Are you sure?'

'Hold it, uhm, yes, the other one's vanished, just like the one in this room!'

'Is that one door busted open too?' Plaintly asked.

'Let's see,' said Lurma, looking yet again. 'No. But it's hanging from just one hinge.'

Symon grunted. 'Sounds busted to me.'

'That's because you can't see what I see,' Lurma snapped. 'I can see the latches. There's two of them and both look to be in perfect working condition. I'd have to pick them both if the door wasn't hanging from just one bent hinge. So don't go telling me my business, Symondenalian!'

'Sorry, Lurma,' said Symon. 'I'm just nervous, and why wouldn't I be, since I'm the only one armed, meaning you're all relying on me to cut through whatever comes at us. And that's my business, Lurma, so shut up about it!'

'All our talents are meshing perfectly,' said Plaintly. 'Okay, Lurma. Great work. Let's go check those open cells.'

'Cells? Who arrested me? I ain't going—oh, don't arrest me!' Barunko burst into tears.

Ophal glanced at the king's manservant, who wandered off to one side to pour himself a massive tankard of wine. He quickly downed three mouthfuls. Stood blinking, licking his lips, only to suddenly totter, reaching out to lean against the wall. Then he smiled, as if at some private joke.

King Bauchelain sat on his throne. 'Ambassador,' he said by way of greeting, 'are you well? Very good. So here we are again, another late night meeting. Fortunately, it is my nature to prowl the span of night, although in this instance, and in the wake of conjurations, bindings and whatnot, I do admit to being somewhat weary. Given that, do be quick about it, will you?'

Tyrants, Ophal decided, loved to listen to themselves talk. 'Prrlll, gweetings, Thire.' He drew out his Imperial missive and began reading, 'To King Bauchelain and to the thitizens of Fair Farwog on the Wiver, after the untheasing prowocationth upon our peathful trade, carawanth and carawantherai, after the egwegiouth pwoclamation of Holy War upon the Wealm of Nightmawia, after the thucthethion of inthults and unwemitting therieth of hateful inthitationth, herrrwenow let it be known that a thtate of war exithth between Nightmawia and Farwog—'

'How delightful,' interjected the king. 'We were wondering when you'd get around to it. I should inform you that Grand General Pin Dollop has assembled an elite force of formidable legions and is even now preparing to march to your mountain realm, there to slaughter and burn your civilization to ash.'

'Yeth,' Ophal nodded. 'However, prrllmit me to inforrrm you that our thpieth are well aware of your pwepawationth, and that Nightmawia, in antithipathion of thith impending *hsssp thvlah* conflict, hath not only athembled the Thoutherrrn Imperial Army, but ith awready on the march. *Fllapp prrlll thlup!*'

'Ah, well then, we shan't have to march as far then, to wipe out your measly horde of scaly lizards.'

Ophal frowned. 'Thcaly Withards?'

'Or is the epithet "Fiend" a more palatable descriptive?'

'Ahh, *prrrl*. Not "Fiend," Thire. "Firrrwend."'

Bauchelain frowned. 'Excuse me?'

'Firrwend, the name of the people of Nightmawia.'

From the wall, the manservant seemed to choke on his wine, hacking out a cough as his face reddened.

After a moment, Bauchelain waved a hand. 'Fiend or Firrwend. Unhuman either way.'

Ophal shook his head. 'Thadly, Thire, no.' He gestured somewhat embarrassedly at himself. 'Unfortunate thkin aiwlllment, awath, thuffithientwy abhorrwent to my fellow thitithenth that I wath thent to the motht wemote wethidence pothible. Thaddled with but one therwant, and but one Impewial Methenger.'

The manservant's coughing worsened and a glance over showed the old man sagging helplessly against the wall.

Ophal shrugged at the king. 'Mithchanth of birrrth, poor Ophal, cweft of pawate, dithjointed of jaw, thenthitive to wight and dryneth, thuth wequirrring thick humidity, dank and darrrk, forrr comforrrt.' The Ambassador shrugged again. 'Motht twagic that I thould love petth in my company, ath I mutht thettle forrr toadth, snakth, worrrmth and the wike. Of dethent company, ahh, *prrrl*, poor Ophal mutht make peath with thowitude.'

King Bauchelain had leaned back and was now stroking his fine beard. 'I see,' he murmured. 'Now then.' He sat forward. 'This Imperial Army of yours . . .'

'Twenty-four wegionth, eighty thouthand heawy infantwy, twellwe thouthand cavalllwy, twellwe thiege engineth, eighteen twebuchetth, two wegionth Imperialll Thapperth, the Royalll Cadwe of High Mageth and Withardth of the Ninth Orrrderrr. Thith forrrce, conthituting the Thoutherrrn Awmy of Nightmawia, ith ewen now cwothing yourrr borrrder and thould be at yourrr wallth in two dayth. *Prrrl, flp!*'

'I take it, then,' said King Bauchelain, 'that reopening peaceful negotiations are out of the question.'

'Alath, too wate, Thire. Motht unfortunate, yeth?'

Bauchelain then raised a long, thin finger. 'A question, sir, if only to satisfy my personal curiosity. Your realm's name, Nightmaria . . .'

'Yeth, welll, what betterrr name to keep unwanted foreignerrrth out of ourrr terrrwitowy?'

'So, in truth, you've been milking that dread reputation, and, one might conclude, in no hurry to disavow the appellation of "Fiend" either?'

Ophal shrugged for a third time. 'Wegretth arrre cheap.'

'Hmm, I see,' said King Bauchelain. 'Mister Reese?'

The manservant started slapping his own face. 'Aye, Master, get the carriage ready. I'm on it.'

Tiny Chanter stepped around a corner and grunted as a man nearly as big as he was stumbled into him. An instant later, with an echoing bellow, the man swung his fist. The *crack* of that fist impacting Tiny's prodigious jaw was a complicated mélange of breaking bone, popping teeth, splitting lip and spraying blood. Eyes rolling up to examine his own brain, Tiny collapsed.

Still bellowing, the stranger now ploughed down the steps, fists flying. Shartorial's nose broke with a crunching sound. Steck Marynd bulled forward, attempting to grapple, only to meet a knee under his jaw that lifted him from his feet. In falling backward, he landed on Apto Canavalian, thus sparing the critic any of the stranger's attention, as he leapt over the jumble of four tumbling, intertwined bodies, and hammered into both Midge and Flea. Biting, punching, kneeing, gouging, the three men fell in a heap, rolling down the stairs.

Shrieking, Brash Phluster leapt high. While this sent him above and thus clear of the tumbling bodies, it also slammed the top of his head into the ceiling. The impact closed his teeth about his tongue with a loud snap, cutting that tongue clean in half.

In the meantime, the wrestling mob reached Tulgord Vise, who had been staring slack-jawed. The impact took him across the shins, breaking both legs. Howling, he collapsed onto the others, although his interest in fighting was likely minimal at the moment.

Even as Apto pushed aside Steck Marynd's unconscious body and clambered upright, a knife hissed past, less than a hand's breadth from his face. It caught Brash Phluster on the way back down from the ceiling, sinking deep into his right shoulder. His scream was a throaty gurgle that erupted in a red cloud.

An instant later, strangers were rushing down the stairs, led by a cross-eyed woman who kept caroming off the walls to either side. They stepped on everyone in their mad rush down and past the escaped prisoners. Blinking, confused, Apto stared after them.

He saw the still-bellowing attacker now rise over the battered forms of Midge, Flea and Tulgord Vise, and then, with a blubbering bawl, set off after his friends.

Gasping, Apto sank down to sit on the steps.

Shartorial Infelance sat up opposite him, holding her mashed nose.

'That looks painful,' said Apto. 'Had I a handkerchief, Milady . . .'

She shook her head, gingerly, and then said, 'Most kind, sir.'

'Were they . . . guards?'

'I think not. But some were, uh, known to me. Thieves.'

'Thieves? Down here? Whatever for?'

'The King, he arrested Dam Loudly Heer, the Head of the Thieves' Guild. I suspect they have come to affect her rescue.'

'Right, but, uh, there's nobody down there. In the crypts, I mean.'

She nodded, but said nothing more.

Steck Marynd groaned where he was lying sprawled on the steps. Farther down, Brash Phluster had found his tongue and was cradling it in his lap as he wept. Someone had pulled the knife from his shoulder, but as there was no-one down there still conscious, Apto assumed that whoever had thrown the knife had retrieved it in passing.

Apto gestured, 'Look down there, Milady. At least one mercy in all this.'

'Excuse me?'

'That poet will never sing again.'

She frowned above her blood-smeared hand. 'You are most cruel, sir.'

'Me? Have you heard him sing?'

A voice quavered down from the stairs above. 'Is Tiny dead? Tiny feels dead. Are these Tiny's teeth? These look like Tiny's teeth.'

'Good thing you took point, Tiny,' called up Apto. 'Otherwise, who knows what might've happened!'

'Tiny hates critics.'

They stumbled into a room, collapsed exhausted to the floor. Barunko had ceased his blubbering, and now sat wiping his eyes and nose, his hands glistening in the faint torchlight.

Slowly regaining her breath, Plaintly set her back against a stone wall. 'Great work, Barunko,' she finally managed.

'They scared me,' said Barunko, knuckling his eyes. 'Came out of nowhere, right in front and there I was, right in front, too. It was like, the two of us, face to face, and his face was so . . . so ugly! I had to punch it, I couldn't help it!'

Lurma suddenly bumped against Plaintly. 'Shh!' she hissed. 'We're not alone!'

'What?' Plaintly looked up, and her eyes narrowed on the tall fat man in the brocaded robes who stood near a floor-to-ceiling cabinet on the other side of the chamber. The man was frowning as he studied the Party of Five.

Symon The Knife hissed, 'Mortari, give me my knife, damn you!'

'I got it,' said Mortari, crawling over. 'I took it out of that man's shoulder! Did you see me do that? Oh, throw it again!'

'Damn you, Symon,' said Lurma, 'if only you had two knives, you could take them both down!'

'There's only the one,' said Le Groutt.

'What? Is there? Oh! Where did the other one go?'

'It's the fucking Grand Bishop,' said Le Groutt.

Symon readied his knife and then threw it. The weapon struck the wall near the ceiling. It fell to the floor in two pieces.

'Shit!' cursed Symon.

'Here, try this,' said Le Groutt, pushing the coil of rope into The Knife's hands. 'Tie him up or something!'

The Grand Bishop then spoke, his voice thin and querulous. 'Who are you? What do you want?'

Plaintly climbed to her feet. 'We're the Party of Five, that's who we are!'

'But there's six of you.'

'What?' Plaintly looked at the others and then said, 'No, there's five, can't you count?'

'That's right,' said Le Groutt. 'Five. The priest's fucking illiterate.'

'No,' said Lurma, 'there's ten of us. I always thought it a strange title—'

'You're in my Chamber of Collections,' said the Grand Bishop. 'I didn't invite you.'

'Never mind that shit,' said Plaintly. 'We're here for the Head of the Thieves' Guild, and we're not leaving without her!'

The round-faced man's brow wrinkled slightly, and then with a shrug he turned and opened the cabinet and collected a severed head from one of the shelves crowded with dozens of other severed heads. Gripping it by the hair he held it out. 'Here, then.'

Plaintly gaped. 'But that's—that's—that's—'

'The head of the Thieves' Guild,' said the Grand Bishop. 'Wasn't that the one you wanted?'

'Hey!' cried Le Groutt, 'where's the rest of her?'

Squinting, Barunko added, 'She's shorter than I remember her. I think. I don't really remember her at all. Is that her? She's short!'

The Bishop frowned. 'Do you want it or don't you? Oh, and did you happen to meet a demon prince? We lost him down here. Him and the Indifferent God, and now we're running out of time.' He set the head down on a table and then brushed his pudgy white hands. 'I have to go.'

Plaintly licked dry lips and then looked about, quickly, before saying, 'Le Groutt, collect that head, will you? We're getting out of here.'

The Grand Bishop then departed through a secret door in the wall behind him.

Lurma leapt to her feet. 'Come on,' she said, 'let's take the other one!' And she sprinted forward until she slammed into a wall, where she slumped to the floor, unconscious.

Frowning, Plaintly said, 'Barunko, pick up Lurma. We can't be waiting around down here any longer, not with a demon prince wandering around!'

Barunko rose to his feet. 'Pick up Lurma. Where?'

'Mortari, guide him over, will you?'

Grumbling, Mortari walked up to Barunko, who grasped him suddenly and flung him into a wall. 'Did he reach the hook?'

'No,' said Plaintly, 'that was earlier, Barunko. Now we just need you to carry Lurma and Mortari.'

'Why, what's wrong with them? Are they dead?'

'Unconscious,' explained Plaintly. 'Le Groutt here will take you to them.'

'Okay,' said Barunko. 'Carry them out. Got it. Le Groutt? Who's got my wrist? Let go!'

'No!' cried Plaintly, 'don't—'

But it was too late, as Barunko punched Le Groutt, sending the man to the floor in a heap.

'Okay,' said Plaintly. 'Barunko, you just stand there, and Symon will drag them over to you, all right?'

'All right. Got it. Drag who?'

'Lurma and Mortari and, uh, Le Groutt. Think you can carry all three of them?'

'Carry? Not sure,' said Barunko. 'I mean, if Barunko was here, why, I bet he could!'

'You're Barunko, Barunko,' said Plaintly.

'Okay, good, hey there's bodies all around me!'

'That's Symon pushing them closer,' said Plaintly, 'so now all you have to do is pick them up one by one.'

Symon turned to Plaintly. 'Le Groutt can't carry the head anymore, Plaintly. Who should take it now?'

'Well,' said Plaintly, 'since you lost your knife, why don't you?'

'Damn,' said Symon, 'I should never have broken that knife.'

'That's how it goes on a mission like this one,' said Plaintly. 'Nothing seems to go as planned and then, all of a sudden, it's mission accomplished! Now all we have to do is evade the demon prince and the Indifferent God, and all those other demons and those headless things.'

'I've got three bodies here,' said Barunko. 'What do you want me to do with them?'

'Just carry them,' said Plaintly. 'Symon, you got her head?'

'I got it, and since her hair's real long, I could swing her like a weapon, maybe even spin round and round and throw her.

You know, this could be better than any knife! Symondenalian The Head Niksos!'

'Smart thinking, Symon,' said Plaintly. 'All right then, take the lead, will you? Barunko's right behind you, and then it's me taking up the rear.'

'Watch out for that darkness behind you, Plaintly,' said Symon. 'It's been chasing us all night!'

'I will, Symon, thanks for reminding me. Now let's get going!'

Ophal D'Neeth Flatroq stepped out through the side postern gate and paused to brush at his green silks. All things considered, the audience had gone rather well, he decided. Formal proclamation announced and here he was, still in possession of his head. Indeed, it occurred to him that he might have to revise his notions regarding maniacal tyrants, as King Bauchelain had proved surprisingly polite, and not in any way inclined to either foam at the mouth or enact highly unjust but altogether expected punishment to the hapless messenger delivering unwelcome news.

Unfortunately for the citizens of Farrog, the approaching forces of Nightmaria weren't much interested in anything but the thorough sacking of the city, the slaughter of its modest army, and the ousting of both the Church of the Indifferent God and the new Royal Line of King Bauchelain, the latter two as messily as possible.

Of course, it seemed likely that neither the king nor his grand bishop would be found anywhere in the city once the defenses collapsed and raging Firends ran amok through the streets. This at least was consistent with his assessment of tyrants. When the dung hits the wall, why, the source of all incumbent misery and suffering has long-since hightailed it out of harm's way.

Typical. He wondered, as he made his way back to the embassy, if there existed some high, impregnable keep, situated atop a mountain or on an isolated island in a sea swarming with savage beasts, where all tyrants fled to as soon as the inevitable occurred. If so, why, wouldn't it be a wonderful thing to, say, drop a whole other mountain on top of them? Crushing into paste every last one!

Slithering along dank alleys, creeping against moss-gummed walls, crossing foul trenches, he came at last to the embassy. Producing a key, he let himself in through the well-hidden back door, and then made his way to where waited the Royal Messenger.

The man was covered in spider webs and dozing on a settee.

Ophal cleared his throat, although that merely produced a strange hissing sound. Still, that proved sufficient, as Beetle Praata flinched upright, blinking owlishly in the gloom.

He started clawing strands of web from his face. 'Ambassador! It is a relief to see you again.'

'*Prrlll*, yeth, fank you. Now, my fwend, we must pweepare to *prrlll* deparrrth, ath the wocalllth willl be motht angwy with uth, yeth?'

Beetle nodded. 'I shall inform the stabler, then, to ready us some mounts.'

'*Prrlll, flip thvlah!* Vewy good. In the meantwime, I thalll deth-twoy documenth and whatnot.'

'It is sad, is it not, Ambassador, that you must quit this city. Please, sir, do not deem this a failure on your part—the Council and the Emperor wish to make that as clear as possible. You did your best.'

'Fank you, sir. Motht kind of you. Thuch a welief!'

Beetle Praata dipped his head in a bow and then strode from the chamber.

In the yard outside the Royal Messenger found Puny Sploor

collapsed against the carcass of his horse. The man was weeping, his small hands curled tight into fists with which he beat weakly and futilely on the dead animal's well-groomed flank. A bucket of water had been dragged up beside the horse's mouth, along with a few handfuls of straw.

Beetle frowned down at the stabler. 'You should know by now,' he said, 'there's no point trying to feed and water a dead horse. Now then, Puny, we have to flee the city. Ready the remaining horses, with saddles upon three of them. The Ambassador will be here shortly.'

Puny Sploor blinked up at Beetle, and then with a shriek he launched himself at the messenger, fingers closing about Beetle's throat.

'Tiny can grow as many new teeth as he wants,' said Tiny, still sitting on the stone steps. 'Tiny has been attacked by demons before.'

'That wasn't a demon,' said Steck Marynd from two steps down, his hands at his temples and a pool of vomit between his feet.

'Tiny says it was a demon, so it was a demon, right Midge?'

'Demon,' said Midge, still trying to push his right eyeball back into its socket, but it kept popping back out. 'Midge can see up his own nose.'

Flea leaned close to his brother. 'Can you see up mine, Midge?'

'I could always see up yours, Flea.'

'But now it must be different, right?'

Midge nodded. 'Different.'

'Better?'

'Maybe.'

Flea smiled.

Apto had ripped a strip from his filthy tunic and given it to Shartorial, to help stop the blood flowing from her broken nose. Now he said, 'The problem is the Mortal Sword's broken legs. He needs splints, or at least binding, if Tiny or Flea are to carry him.'

'Tiny carries no-one,' said Tiny. 'Midge and Flea don't neither. The fool can crawl for all Tiny cares.'

'Fub fab bib,' said Brash Phluster, and then he burst into tears again.

'There is a cutter's room,' said Shartorial Infelance, 'containing the Royal Apothecary. Healing salves, unguents and some High Denul elixirs. It's not far.'

Brash leapt to his feet, eyes fervent with sudden hope. He still held his severed tongue.

Apto sighed, 'Right, I suppose we'll have to make for that then. But Tulgord still needs help to get him there, and I have a bad back and all. It's a chronic condition, had it since, uh, since birth.'

Groaning, Steck Marynd straightened. 'I will carry him, then. With luck, he'll pass out with the pain.'

'Pass out?' Tulgord glowered up at Steck. 'More like die!'

'Pray to your goddess for salvation, sir,' advised Steck, making his way down the steps. 'I'll be as gentle as possible, but I make no promises.'

'There is mercy in your soul, sir,' said Tulgord Vise, grudgingly.

'Tiny can grow as many new teeth as he wants. Tiny has been attacked by demons before.'

'You said that just a moment ago,' Apto pointed out.

'Tiny never repeats himself. Never.'

'I think you're addled.'

'Tiny's not addled. The world is addled. That's why the walls are leaking and his fingernails are buzzing.'

Amidst grunts, yelps, groans and moans, Steck Marynd worked Tulgord Vise onto his back, gripping the man's thick wrists. This meant the legs dangled and bounced along the steps, and after a few moments of this, Tulgord Vise passed out.

'Lead on, Milady,' rasped Steck Marynd.

Nodding, she resumed the journey up the stairs, Apto right behind her followed by the Chanters and then Brash Phluster behind them with Steck and Tulgord taking up the rear.

'Might get your tongue back, Phluster,' said Apto, 'proving the universe's essential indifference to justice.'

'Buh ovv,' the poet replied.

They reached a landing and Shartorial led them through a doorway, down another passageway, through another doorway and then went left at a T-intersection, coming at last to a final door. 'We're here,' she said, turning the latch and swinging it open.

Crowded inside were thirty-two demons. Sixty-three eyes fixed upon the newcomers, and then in a collective roar, the demons attacked.

Apto grasped hold of Shartorial and pulled her behind the door as the swarm poured out in a shrieking, slavering mob.

Bellowing, the Chanters vanished beneath a mound of writhing, spitting, snarling, biting, clawing creatures. Farther down the corridor, Steck was dragging Tulgord into a side-passage, Brash Phluster trying to push past them.

Apto risked a peek into the chamber. 'It's clear!' he hissed, dragging Shartorial around and inside, whereupon he slammed shut the door. 'That was close!'

'But Steck—'

'Made his escape, Milady, I promise you! I saw it with my own eyes!' He paused, and then said, 'But if the demons followed, well, he's finished. Dead. The poet too. In fact, Milady, we're probably the last ones left.'

Beyond the door the demons were now screaming along with the Chanters. Bodies struck walls, the floor, the ceiling and the door itself, the meaty impacts rattling the thick planks and popping bronze rivets.

'Sounds lively out there,' said Apto, offering Shartorial a modest smile. 'But I judge us safe, at least for the next little while.'

The door opened and Tiny barged into the Apothecary with three demons clinging to him and more rushing in behind.

Apto shrieked, grasping Shartorial Infelance and pushing her forward. 'It's all her fault! Not me! Not me!'

'Ah,' said Bauchelain as he adjusted his cloak, 'here he is. Korbal Broach old friend, are you well?'

The Grand Bishop stepped into the courtyard and looked round. 'I think it's going to rain,' he said, peering up at the night sky and sniffing.

'Quite possible,' Bauchelain agreed.

'Your Demon Prince has escaped.'

'Yes well, these things happen. What of your god?'

'Gone, too.'

'No matter. As you can see, Mister Reese has made us ready to depart this ungrateful city and its humorless neighbors. Our carriage awaits, as it were.'

'There is an army coming,' said Korbal Broach. 'I can feel them. With many powerful sorcerors. They are all very angry. Why are they angry, Bauchelain?'

'Misapprehensions, alas, for which I have decided to blame Grand General Pin Dollop.'

'Shall I kill him for you?' Korbal Broach asked.

'Alas, he has already led his army out of the city and will momentarily march straight into the maw of the punitive

Firrwend forces. I would imagine he'll not survive the encounter.'

'Oh. Good.'

'Indeed,' said Bauchelain as he drew on his leather gloves. 'It comforts, does it not, when justice is seen to be served. Mister Reese.'

Emancipor was leaning against the tall front wheel of the carriage. 'Yes, Master?'

'The Royal Treasury.'

'With all the other loot, Master, in that clever Warren you created beneath the floorboards. You know,' he added, 'I've been dumping stuff in there for years now.'

'Mmhmm, yes?'

'Well, I was just wondering, Master, when is enough enough?'

Bauchelain turned to face him, one thin brow arching. 'Dear me, Mister Reese. Very well, allow me to explain. Ideally, one—in this case yours truly—envisages a world with a single, indeed global, economy, wherein wealth flows from all quarters in a seemingly ceaseless river, or series of rivers, all gathering in one particular place, that place being, of course, my coffers.'

'Huh,' said Emancipor Reese.

'Like a massive body bearing a million small cuts, the blood draining into a single gutter.'

'And, er, you're the gutter then?'

'Precisely.'

'But what about everyone else, Master? The ones trying to make enough to live well, or even enough to eat and maybe raise a family?'

'Accord them no sympathy, Mister Reese. They make their own fate, after all, and if through incompetence, laziness or stupidity they must live a life of abject suffering and hopeless, despairing misery, why, no-one ever said the world was fair. In the meantime,' he added with a faint sigh, 'it falls to the capable ones, such as me, to bleed the suckers dry. And then to convince them—given their innate stupidity it proves rather easy, by the way—of just how fortunate they are that I am running things.'

'Aye, sir, sly as a fox you are, that's for sure.'

'I am not sure, Mister Reese, if I like the comparison. Foxes are often the prey of frenzied packs of dogs let loose by the in-bred classes, after all. I do not see myself as the object of such sport.'

'Sport, huh? Aye, Master. My apologies, then.'

'Now, Mister Reese, I think it best we take our leave. Korbal, dearest, will you ensure the path before us is unobstructed all the way to the South Gate?'

'Okay.'

Emancipor prepared to climb up to the driver's bench, but then he glanced over at Bauchelain. 'Master, just one thing's got me wondering.'

'Yes?'

'All that loot, sir. You never seem to use any of it.'

'Well of course not, Mister Reese. I simply wish to *possess* it, thereby exercising my absolute power in preventing anyone else from ever using it. In fact, my special Warren is designed in such a manner that there are no exits from it. What goes in stays in. Unless I choose otherwise. I point this out to make certain you do not concoct any grand deception, or thievery, although I remain confident of your loyalty.'

'Uh, right. Thank you, Master. I had no plans in that direction.'

'I didn't think you had, Mister Reese. Now then, I believe Korbal Broach is ready?'

Korbal Broach nodded. 'Yes, Bauchelain. Everybody I've killed and worked on since we got here is now in the street outside.'

'Ah, excellent . . . yes, I think I hear the screaming begin. Mister Reese?'

Emancipor gathered the traces. The four black horses, their hides steaming as was their wont, lifted their heads, mouths opening as they sank their fangs into the bits, eyes flaring a lurid, blazing amber. He flicked the straps. 'Move along now,' he said, making clicking noises.

Mortari's head was now swollen on the other side, but Plaintly Grasp was relieved to see him smiling. Le Groutt's jaw had been unhinged by Barunko's punch and was shifted well off to one side, so that the lower half of his face was misaligned with the upper half. He could now close his mouth with nary a single clack of teeth, a trick that made even Barunko giggle.

Lurma Spilibus had also regained consciousness and was even now creeping stealthily towards the postern door they had passed through earlier that night. Watching Lurma slip from side to side in the narrow corridor filled Plaintly with an almost overwhelming sense of well-being.

'Another successful mission by the Party of Five,' she said, glancing at Symon The Head Niksos. 'Into the very palace itself and back out again! Another legend to our name, friends. I don't know why we ever split up in the first place.'

'Artistic differences,' said Symon. 'Overblown egos, too much drugs and hard liquor.'

'No,' Plaintly said, scowling, 'that's what ruined The Seven Thieves of The Baker's Dozen and the Fancy Pillagers.'

'And the Masons, too,' added Barunko.

Symon frowned. 'What masons?'

'The Grand High Order of the Wax Masons,' said Barunko, rolling up a sleeve to reveal a tattoo of a bee on his forearm. 'I was Chief Rumpah of the Lavender Hive of the Full Moon.'

'You were a Honeymooner?' Symon asked, eyes widening. 'I never knew!'

'Once a month at the third bell before midnight,' said Barunko, 'I ate a basketful of lavender flowers and then bared my ass to the heavens, letting out aromatic farts—none of the others could fart as many times as me! That's when the jealousy started, and Borbos started sneaking in lima beans and cabbage to try and beat me so I had to kill him, right? Since he was a cheater! And besides, his farts were killing bees!'

'You had a whole secret life!' Symon accused Barunko. 'And you didn't tell any of us!'

Barunko blinked sleepily. 'Everything masons do is secret. That's the whole point of it. Being, uh, secret. And secretive, and keeping secrets, too. I drink a bottle of d'bayang oil every day to keep me from knowing my own secrets! I think,' he added, 'it's wearing off.'

'How can you tell?' Symon asked.

'Well, I can see straight, for one.'

Lurma hissed impatiently from the door and then waved them over.

'Granma used to keep a kitten up her—'

'Not now, Mortari!' hissed Lurma, scowling, 'I can hear a crowd out there! In the street! They're partying or something—did we miss a fête? Never mind, we need to slink out, quiet like, so nobody notices us, and just blend in with the crowd, in case guards are watching or something.'

'Our last challenge,' said Plaintly. 'We can do it! The Party of Five went and retrieved the Head of the Thieves' Guild! Imagine that!'

'Actually,' said Barunko, 'There's six of us, provided you count yourself, too.'

'What?' Plaintly stared at Barunko.

'Never mind. Let's get out of here. I'm getting the shakes.'

Lurma fumbled for the latch for a moment, found it at last, and then edged open the door. Plaintly pushed Le Groutt forward, and then Mortari. 'Symon, have that head ready just in case,' she whispered, nudging him past her. 'Barunko, take up the rear.'

Barunko let out a loud fart, and then shrugged. 'Sorry, what you said was a code phrase. It's all coming back.'

Plaintly reeled against the wall. 'Hood's wind, Barunko, what have you been eating?'

'It's the D'bayang oil, Plaintly. You can't really drink it straight. Instead, you fill the bottle with slugs and let them soak it all up, then you swallow down the slugs.'

'That's what I'm smelling all right,' nodded Plaintly. 'Slug farts! I thought it was familiar. Now, stay right behind me, will you, as we make our way through the crowd.'

Barunko nodded.

Heart thudding with excitement, Plaintly slipped through the doorway after the others, and out into the street.

She caught a momentary glimpse of Symon, screaming soundlessly as he fought with a headless undead. Both had a grip on Dam Loudly Heer's head, and then Plaintly saw that the headless body was Dam Loudly Heer herself. Then she saw that almost the entire mob consisted of undead, most of them headless though a few sported two, even three heads, artlessly sewn onto shoulders. Still other figures were writhing jumbles of arms and legs, sprouting from mangled torsos. In the midst of this seething crowd were citizens shrieking in panic, along with palace guards busy getting their armor torn off, ears ripped off and eyes gouged from the sockets. Here and there swords swung, punctuated by meaty thuds or shocked screams; spears jabbed, fists flew, pitchforks stabbed—Barunko pushed past her. 'It's a fête!' he shouted, wading in.

'No, Barunko! Wait!'

To her utter astonishment, Barunko turned.

'We've got to gather the others! Get us all to cover! Anywhere! We've got to get out of this!'

He frowned, and then nodded. 'Okay. Follow me!'

There were dead demons everywhere. Bruised, bloody and exhausted, Tiny stood glowering, flanked by Flea and a one-eyed Midge, who now had a collection of eyeballs cupped in one hand and was poking them about, presumably looking for the right one.

Steck Marynd, with Tulgord Vise on his back, finally appeared in the doorway, and Shartorial—now mostly naked after her spat with a few demons—rushed towards him. Behind them all, Brash Phluster slipped round and stumbled into the Apothecary, heading straight for the shelves at the back of the room and their rows of phials, flasks, bottle and jars.

Apto straightened what was left of his prisoner's tunic. 'That was hairy,' he said. 'If not for my bad back I'd have joined in the slaughter. I'm sure you're all aware of that—'

Shartorial had said something—something probably unflattering regarding Apto—and now Steck Marynd carefully set Tulgord Vise down, straightened, and walked towards the critic.

Who backed away. 'What's wrong, sir? Look at us—we all made it out alive! There's nothing—she's lying! Whatever she said is a lie!'

'Don't kill critic,' said Tiny. 'Tiny kills critic.'

Steck paused and glanced back. 'Not this time. This time, Steck Marynd will see justice done—'

'No! Tiny sees justice! Done!'

At the back of the chamber, Brash Phluster pushed into his mouth the piece of gray meat that had once been the front half of his tongue, and then started guzzling one bottle after another. He choked, gagged, coughed out the meat, stuffed it back in and resumed drinking.

'Look at the poet!' Apto cried.

Everyone turned.

Apto rushed past them all, back into the corridor, where he ran for his life. He heard angry shouts behind him. He found another corridor, pelted down it, and then, at the end of a short side passage, he found another set of stairs. At the threshold he paused. Up? No! They would expect that! Down! Down he ran.

Very faintly, from somewhere above, he heard Flea say, 'I thought he had a bad back!'

Apto laughed nastily. Then stumbled, fell, bounced and flounced wildly down the steps, and finally came to a rest on a landing, or, perhaps, the lowest level. In agony, he lay gasping in the darkness, and then heard something shuffling towards him. Panic gripped him. 'What's that? Who's there? Leave me alone. I only ever speak the objective truth! Not my fault if I crushed your love of doing art, or whatever! Was it me who cut off your head? No! Listen, I own a villa and it's all yours! I promise!'

There was a low, weak chuckle, and then a demon's drawn, ashen face loomed over Apto Canavalian. The demon grinned. 'I remember you,' it said. 'From Crack'd Pot Trail.'

'No! Not possible! We've never met, I swear it!'

The demon's smile broadened. 'You've caught the attention of the Indifferent God. Very rare gift, this meeting here, oh, yes, very rare!' It held up a flaccid length of knobby, bruised meat that dripped from both ends. 'Look, I used it so much it fell off. Mother warned me but did I listen?'

'I'm sorry, what?'

'But I bet you have one. Should last me a week or two, easy.'

Apto suddenly laughed. 'You're wrong there! I've just broken my spine! I can't feel a thing from below the neck! Hah hah hah, you lose!'

The possessed demon scowled. 'Truly?'

'Truth! In fact, I've never been more spineless than I am right now!'

'Now you lie!'

'All right,' Apto admitted, 'that was perhaps an exaggeration. But that doesn't change anything. I broke my back, and I'll probably die right here, lost and abandoned by all my friends. It's a horrible way to go, and you know, if you were a merciful god, you'd—'

'Kill you? But I'm not a merciful god, am I?'

'You're not? Oh, damn. I'm doomed, then.'

The demon's face split into a wide grin again. 'Yes, you are. That's right, no audience for you! All alone! Forgotten! Discarded!' The demon pulled back, began shuffling away. 'Need,' it whispered, 'to find another. Another . . . oh me, oh my, Mother was right! Why didn't I listen? I never listen, oh why? Why?'

Apto listened to its whining dwindle, and then, finally, all was silence.

He sat up. 'Shit,' he muttered, 'that was close.'

'It worked!' cried Brash Phluster. 'It worked! I can talk again! And sing! Aaalahh la la lah leeee!'

'Tiny tear out his tongue again,' said Tiny. 'Everyone cheers. A standing ovation.'

Brash Phluster snapped his mouth shut and shrank back to cower beneath the shelves.

'We're forgetting why we're here,' said Steck Marynd. 'The Nehemoth.' He turned to Shartorial Infelance. 'Milady? Can you lead us to the throne room?'

'Yes, of course, but I fear there will be many, many guards—'

'On your authority, however?'

She considered, and then nodded. 'Yes, a special audience. But I will need a change of attire if I am to be convincing.'

'I would advise,' said Steck, 'that you do so on your own, and then return here when you are ready.' He glanced at Tulgord Vise. 'That salve is working, but the bones still need more time to properly knit.'

'Soon,' promised the Mortal Sword. 'I can feel the heat of their mending!'

'Very well,' said Shartorial. She then leaned close and kissed Steck Marynd, before rushing out of the room.

Brash Phluster crept out a few steps. 'I will sing of this, Steck Marynd, the love that defied chains, and bars, and locked doors, and the fact that you haven't bathed in weeks and are pretty homely besides.'

'That's not his tongue,' said Midge, 'that's someone else's.'

Brash Phluster shrugged. 'What if it was? There were plenty lying about, and besides, look at that new eye of yours!'

Midge scowled. 'What about it?'

'Well, where did you find the dead goat? Is what I'm wondering.'

'It's a demon's eye!' said Midge. 'And with it I can see demon things!'

'What demon things?' Brash asked.

Midge waved about. 'Things demons can see, of course. That table there, and those chairs.'

'I can see those too.'

'But I see them the way demons do!'

'Well, with one eye at least.'

Midge made a fist. 'Not if I tear out my other eye and find another demon eye!'

'Possibly,' Brash said, and then shrugged, 'though I'm not convinced of that.'

Flea laughed and pointed. 'Look, Tiny, Midge has a goat eye! Ha ha!'

'It's not a goat! It's a demon!'

'Does it even work?' Brash Phluster asked.

Midge slumped. 'It will. Soon.'

'Tiny eats goats for breakfast and demons for lunch. Tiny eats dragons for supper.'

'And then sits on the shit bucket for the rest of the night,' said Brash Phluster.

Steck Marynd snorted, and then eyed the poet curiously. 'Most peculiar. I now wonder what potion you've swallowed, beyond the one miraculously mending your tongue.'

'The Make Tiny Kill Poet potion,' said Tiny.

Brash Phluster sneered. 'This is what an empowered artist is like, Tiny Chanter. No sharper weapon than talent, no crueler eye than that of an artist unleashed. Insult or threaten me again and I'll see you flensed alive, mocked in a thousand songs, aped by ten thousand mummers and twenty thousand clowns. I'll see you—'

'Better cease the threats,' advised Steck Marynd, 'before the witless thug does what all witless thugs do.'

'Which is?' Brash Phluster asked.

'Yes,' said Tiny, 'which is?'

'Why, kill the artist, of course.'

'Yes, this is what Tiny is going to do.'

Brash laughed, 'Really? So, Tiny Chanter, you're a witless thug, are you?'

'Tiny's not witless. Tiny's not a thug. Tiny's not a witless thug either.'

'So you won't be killing me after all?'

Tiny frowned, and then glanced at Midge, but Midge had one hand covering his good eye and was taking baby steps, his other hand held out lest he walk into something unexpected. Tiny then glanced at Flea, who looked back, smiled and waved.

Groaning, Tulgord Vise slowly regained his feet, wincing as he put his full weight on his legs. Then he straightened and let out a heavy sigh. 'Almost ready,' he said.

Shartorial Infelance rushed back into the chamber, wearing a new shimmery dress of creamy silk with rose petal patterns spilling down to the hem, which sat delicately above the tops of her small feet. Her hair was freshly coiffed, too.

'That was . . . amazing,' said Brash Phluster.

'We have a chance!' she said breathlessly, her cheeks pink, her eyes alight, 'there's no guards anywhere!'

Steck Marynd smiled. 'Necromancers garner little loyalty, it seems. As expected. To your weapons, friends, it's time to end this!'

Brash Phluster watched them all rush from the room, and then he turned back to the shelf and began pocketing as many phials and bottles as he could. He hummed under his breath as he did so, and it was a fine hum indeed.

Emancipor cursed as the mob seethed against one side of the carriage. He leaned down towards the speaking tube. 'It's no good, Master! The whole damned city's in the streets! They've torn apart all the monsters!'

The side door opened and out stepped Bauchelain. One gesture cleared a space as bodies went flying. He climbed up beside his manservant and stood looking at the mobbed street ahead.

'I see. How unfortunate. Can you see Korbal Broach?'

'He veered into a crow and flew away, Master.'

'Did he now? Well, to be expected, as he has every confidence in my ability to extricate ourselves from this situation.'

'Glad to hear it,' said Emancipor. 'Uh, exactly how do you plan on doing that, by the way?'

'Well, first of all, I shall set the horses on fire.'

'Oh.'

'Fear not, Mister Reese, they're used to it.'

'Right. That's good, then. And after that?'

'Well, as much as it offends my sensibilities, I shall have to walk ahead and clear for us a path. Shield your gaze as best you can, Mister Reese, as it shall be a messy traverse.' And from somewhere he drew out a midnight blue two-handed sword that then burst into flickering blue flames. 'In this blade,' Bauchelain said, 'are imprisoned a thousand hungry demons, and tonight, Mister Reese, they shall feed unto gluttony.'

'Right, good for them I say. Just get us out of here!'

Bauchelain smiled. 'Why, Mister Reese, whence the source of this admirable self-interest? Most enchanting.'

'Aye, Master, self-interest, that's me all over.'

Bauchelain brandished the sword, the gesture spraying out writhing tongues of blue flame—sufficient to draw some attention, as cries of terror arose on all sides. 'Now then, allow me some room, Mister Reese, and keep tight the traces as you follow along.'

'Aye Master, count on it!'

Bauchelain then leapt down.

And began the terrible slaughter.

Scratched, bitten, and battered, the Party of Five reached the back of the giant black carriage. Lurma Spilibus scrabbled at the latch of the storage trap and, eventually, found it. She then twisted the latch, only to turn her cross-eyed face at Plaintly. 'Locked!'

'Then pick it and hurry up!'

While she set to work, Barunko and Symon fended off wild, panicked citizens, most of whom seemed to be in a strange frenzy and disinclined to reason on this night, while Le Groutt scared people by leering with his misaligned jaw, and Mortari poked at his swollen head with a shard of broken glass, spurting goo at anyone who came too close.

'It's jammed!' said Lurma, 'and now I've broken the pick!'

With a bearish growl, Barunko stepped back, reached round and tore open the trap door.

Plaintly peered in. 'You won't believe this!' she hissed. 'It's full of gold coins and gems and diamonds and bolts of silk and—'

'Let's go!' cried Lurma, and she clambered inside. The others quickly followed. When Barunko, who was last, grunted his way into the narrow space, the trap door slammed shut, leaving them all in utter darkness.

Plaintly listened but only heard lots of harsh breaths and the rustle of coins shifting under them. 'We all here?' she asked. 'Count off!'

Mortari said, 'Me!'

Le Groutt said, 'Eee!'

'I'm here,' said Barunko.

'So am I,' hissed Lurma Spilibus.

'That's it, then!' said Plaintly Grasp. 'We're all here! The Party of Five!'

'No,' said Symon, 'you forgot me!'

'What? Oh, wait, we really *are* the Party of Six!'

'You counted wrong,' said Barunko, 'although you're right. What I mean is, with Symon included, there's six of us, but only if that includes you, Plaintly. Or in my case, me.'

'Why wouldn't you include me?' Plaintly demanded. 'Or you? Anyway, until Symon spoke I counted five, so we must be the Party of Six!'

'Unless,' said Mortari, 'someone else is in here with us!'

Plaintly Grasp tensed. 'Oh gods, we're not alone!'

'No,' said Mortari. 'There's me and Le Groutt and Lurma and . . .'

'I can't find the damned trap door,' said Barunko. 'It was right behind me, I swear!'

'Everyone split up and start looking for the trap door,' said Plaintly.

'Everyone?' asked Mortari.

'Everyone!'

'Even the one who's hiding in here with us?'

'Yes,' said Plaintly, fighting off her panic as she did not like confining spaces. 'Even that one!'

'That means,' said Mortari, 'we're actually the Party of Seven!'

'No, six,' said Plaintly, who wasn't yet convinced of Barunko's argument.

'Eleven,' said Lurma Spillibus.

'Seven,' said a voice no-one recognized.

Traversing empty corridors, crossing abandoned chambers already looted and with stains of blood here and there on the floor, Shartorial Infelance led them at last to the twin doors behind which waited the throne room.

The Nehemothanai began checking weapons, straps and fittings.

'Poet ran away,' said Tiny.

Grunting, Steck Marynd said, 'I'm not surprised. One can only hope that the potion that made him smarter than normal will wear off.'

'Why?' asked Tulgord Vise as he examined the longsword he'd found.

'A man with sufficient wits will likely escape this wretched night with his life,' Steck replied. 'A man with the normal wits of Brash Phluster is much more likely to die, and most horribly, too.'

'You reveal a cruel streak,' observed Tulgord Vise.

Steck Marynd shrugged. 'He'll survive the night, I'm sure. Beyond that, however, well, since when was an artist hard-eyed and silken-tongued enough to tell the truth, of any use to anyone? That man could become an icon of dissent, a lodestone to disenfranchised revolutionaries, the namby-pamby favorite of the worshipping classes of fawners, hangers-on and other assorted miscreants.' He paused as everyone was staring at him, Tiny with a frown, Midge with a scowl that made his demon eye glow, Flea with a wide smile, Tulgord Vise with a thoughtful expression, and Shartorial Infelance with an adoring one.

Suddenly uncomfortable, Steck said, 'I had aspirations to be a weaver of epics, once. It's said, after all, that there's an epic tale in each and every one of us. It's all down to just writing it down, and only the lucky few of us ever find the time away from the necessities of living, socializing, daydreaming and wishful thinking.' He grimaced and stared at a wall. 'Can't be very hard, anyway,' he muttered. 'Look at Brash Phluster, for Hood's sake!' Then, scowling, he shook his head and collected up his crossbow. 'Well, never mind all that shit. We've got some necromancers to kill!'

Shartorial Infelance flung herself onto Steck. 'I knew it!' she cried, loudly planting wet, sloppy kisses to his face. 'Oh, you could be the Century's Greatest Artist, I just know it!'

'Tiny wants to throw up.'

Swearing under his breath, Tulgord Vise stepped forward and kicked open the twin doors to the throne room.

One of the doors collided with something that made a

crunching sound, followed by muffled curses, and an instant later an enormous demon bedecked in supple furs, oiled chain, iron torcs and assorted other accoutrements, staggered into view, clutching its nose which was now streaming blood.

'Bastard!' it groaned, glowing eyes bright with tears.

'Stand aside if you value your life!' Tulgord Vise bellowed.

Blinking, the demon stepped to one side, and then, as the Nehemothanai bulled into the room, it said, 'You're too late if you're after Bauchelain and Korbal Broach.'

'Not again!' cried Tulgord Vise.

Tiny laughed. 'Look! Tiny sees a throne for the taking! Hah ha ha! Hah! Hah ha!'

'Forget it,' said the demon. 'Tried that. It's no good.'

Tiny frowned up at the creature. 'You don't know Tiny Chanter.'

'That's true, I don't. Who is he?'

'This is Tiny Chanter,' said Tiny, thumping his own chest. 'High Mage! D'ivers! King of Toll City of Stratem! Leader of the Nehemothanai! And now king of Farrog, hah!'

'Leader of the Nehemothanai?' snorted Tuglord Vise. 'I take no orders from you, you brainless oaf!'

The demon pointed at the throne. 'We've all been played. Bauchelain left an heir, and woe to the fool who dares challenge him!'

Tiny squinted at the throne. 'Tiny sees nobody!'

'Draw closer, then,' the demon said, smirking.

Tiny crept gingerly forward, eyes darting, ears twitching at the slightest sound to the left and right, real or imagined. When he glanced back over a shoulder, Flea smiled and waved.

Six paces from the throne he halted, stiffened, and then slowly straightened. 'I see a mouse on the cushion!' He looked back at the demon. 'Ha! Hah! Hah hah ha! Ha!'

'A demonic mouse,' said the giant demon. 'Oh yes, beware

Bauchelain's sense of humor. The punchline of every one of his jokes is announced in a welter of blood, guts and messy death!' It gestured dismissively. 'You've been warned, the least I can do. Oh, and by the way, an army is about to crush this city. I wouldn't tarry overlong.'

The demon then fled the throne room.

Tiny continued eyeing the mouse, which in turn had lifted its cute little head, twitching with both its cute little nose with its cute little whiskers.

'Tiny can take it,' said Tiny in a quavering voice.

'Oh,' said Flea, 'it's so cute and little!'

'Heed that demon's words,' advised Steck Marynd. 'Milady,' he said, 'best step back.' He lifted his crossbow. 'This could get messy. But that said, is it not our duty to rid the world of the Nehemoth's minions, no matter where we find them?'

'Then we should all rush it as one,' suggested Tulgord Vise, hefting his sword.

'Once I loose my quarrel, aye,' nodded Steck Marynd. 'You listening, Tiny?'

'Tiny hears you,' said Tiny. 'Its eyes are glowing most fiercely. Do mouse eyes normally glow? Tiny's not sure. Tiny's not sure of anything anymore!'

Flea burst into tears.

Behind them all the double doors suddenly slammed shut, the sound so startling that Steck's finger instinctively flexed, releasing the quarrel.

Straight for the mouse.

Mayhem erupted.

A block away and traversing corpse-strewn streets, Brash Phluster flinched and turned at the sound of the palace's sudden, inexplicable collapse.

He paid the billowing dust and now flames only momentary heed, his mind frantically occupied as it was on the Epic Lay of Brash Phluster, a ten volume, ten million word poem unwaveringly adhering to the classic iambic hexameter in the style of the Lost Droners of Ipscalon.

Visions of glory danced through his forebrain.

Twenty-four paces later, the Potion of Ineluctable Genius wore off. He looked round, shrieked and then ran for the nearest sewer hole.

Part Two

THE NEXT DAY
OUTSIDE FARROG

Beneath the bright light of dawn, Grand General Pin Dollop cursed and then rode out in front of his legions. He wheeled his mount. 'This is our moment!' he cried in his thin, girly voice. 'Those numbers you see behind me are deceiving! Mere conscripts! A peasant army and never mind all that twinkly armor and those big shields! They'll shatter to our hammer blow! Run shrieking for the hills!'

'Shatter!' bellowed his army.

'Yes!' Pin Dollop screamed back.

'Run shrieking for the hills!'

'Exactly! Now, follow me, as we charge into legend!' And he dragged his horse round, set heels to its flanks, and led the wild charge into the mass of ordered legions directly ahead.

This was glory! This was jaw-dropping courage, breathtaking audacity, a charge not just into legend but into the hoary myths that crawled and stumbled their way down through all of history!

His horse tripped over a badger den, throwing the Grand

General from the saddle. He landed in a perfect shoulder roll and lithely regained his feet even as he dragged free his short-sword.

Directly ahead, thirty thousand archers nocked arrows.

Laughing fearlessly, Pin Dollop glanced back—

To see his legions shattered, the soldiers flinging down their weapons and running shrieking for the hills.

He spun back round as thirty thousand arrows arced into the sky, all converging on Pin Dollop.

He ducked.

Well disguised beneath a heavy damp cloak, Ophal D'Neeth Flatroq sat perched upon the high saddle, stroking his pet slow-worm, which he kept covered up lest the sight of it frighten one of countless refugees lining the narrow road.

After some time, he sighed and twisted in the saddle. 'Willl you two thtop gwarrrwing at each other! It wuth awwrll a mithunderthtanding, yeth?'

'He tried to strangle me!' snapped Beetle Praata.

'And he made me groom and water and feed a dead horse!' retorted Puny Sploor.

'Oh, bother! Methenger Beetle, find uth a dank cave for the night, willll you? And you, Puny Thploor, clearrr uth a path thwough thethe wefugeeth!'

'Oh really? And how exactly do I do that?'

'I don't know why I keep you on, to be honetht.'

'You keep me on because I'm the only man in the world who doesn't throw up at the sight of you eating, oh Failed Ambassador of the Burning City of Farrog!'

Well, Ophal conceded, the man had a point there. He gestured with one gloved hand. 'Wellll, do the betht you can, then. And you, Methenger, why are you thtill here? A cave, I thaid!'

'Right,' Beetle growled, taking up his reins. 'Another fucking cave. Right. Got it.' He rode off.

Ophal sighed again. At least Eeemlee his pet slow-worm never complained. He resumed stroking it. Then glanced down to find that it was dead. 'Puny Thploor, betht look away, ath I am hungwy.'

A full day's travel from the city of Farrog and Emancipor could still see, when looking back, the pillar of black smoke. He wiped at his itchy, stinging eyes, and glanced at his master who sat beside him on the bench. 'I have to admit, sir, that I'm glad you didn't have to kill and maim too many of them citizens before the rest broke and ran.'

'Mister Reese, your mercy remains a quaint if somewhat tiresome affectation. For myself, I confess to some disappointment. The demons bound in my sword are very frustrated indeed. We shall have to find us another city, or situation, in which to exercise my obligations to them.'

'Really? When?'

'Oh, not too soon, I assure you.' He lifted a hand and gestured ahead. 'Do you see Korbal there? He rides well the updrafts, wouldn't you agree?'

'I think he prefers being a crow to being a man.'

'On occasion, Mister Reese, I share his bias.'

'Ain't noticed that much of late, Master.'

'Well, it is easier keeping you company this way, Mister Reese, than being a crow balanced upon your rather thin shoulder.'

'All on account of me, huh? Well, I'm, er, flattered.'

'As you should be. That said, you must understand, frustration stalks us, alas. Oh, the endless wealth we steal soothes the soul, to be sure. But the true exercise of power, Mister Reese, ah, so fleeting!'

'Forgiving me being forward and all, Master, but what you two need is a keep somewhere. Impregnable, unassailable, forbidding, suitably haunted.'

'Hmm, a curious notion, Mister Reese. Mind you, do recall Blearmouth. Oh yes, it all started off well, and our wintering there was most enjoyable, until the infernal Nehemothanai caught wind of us. I admit that I grow weary of staying one step ahead of them, in particular that army and the Mysterious Lady commanding them.'

'A strong enough keep, sir,' ventured Emancipor, 'and you'd not have to worry.'

'You appear to share our weariness in this endless journey.'

'Well, Master, it's all the same to me, to be honest.'

'Perhaps if Korbal Broach assembled an army of undead . . .'

'That'd be fine, sir, if they weren't so, uh, useless.'

'Granted, although I warn you not to venture such opinions within hearing of my erstwhile comrade.'

'Not me, sir. Never. Not a chance.'

'Now, Mister Reese, I well see your exhaustion. Do retire to the confines of the carriage and get yourself some sleep. I can manage the traces for a time, I assure you.'

'Thank you, sir,' Emancipor said, handing the traces over to his master. He stretched out the kinks in his back. 'I'll just have me a pipe first, then, by way of relaxing and whatnot.'

'Best be quick,' Bauchelain advised. 'I am of a mind to take this carriage into a warren, to traverse the wild raging flames of some nether realm, if only to confuse our trail.'

Emancipor stuffed the pipe back into its pouch and made for the carriage door. 'I can smoke later,' he said hastily.

'As you will, Mister Reese. Now then, you may hear the horses screaming. Pay that no mind. They're used to it.'

Emancipor paused at the door. 'Aye, sir, and so am I.'

ABOUT THE AUTHOR

Steven Erikson is an archaeologist and anthropologist—and the author of one of the defining works of Epic Fantasy: The Malazan Book of the Fallen, which has been hailed 'a masterwork of the imagination.' The first novel in this astonishing ten-book series, *Gardens of the Moon*, was short-listed for the World Fantasy Award. He has also written a number of novellas set in the same fantasy world and *Willful Child*, an affectionate parody of a long-running science fiction television series. *Forge of Darkness* begins the Kharkanas Trilogy—a series which takes readers back to the origins of the Malazan world. *Fall of Light* continues this epic tale. Steven Erikson lives in Victoria, Canada.

Printed in the USA
CPSIA information can be obtained
at www.ICGtesting.com
LVHW021240070324
773798LV00003B/386